M000040278

Magdalena Tulli

Dreams and Stones

Translated by Bill Johnston

archipelago books

First Archipelago Edition, 2004
First Archipelago Paperback Edition, 2015

Library of Congress Cataloging-in-Publication Data
Tulli, Magdalena.
[Sny i kamienie. English]
Dreams and Stones / by Magdalena Tulli ;
translated from the Polish by Bill Johnston. – 1st ed.
p. cm.
ISBN 0-9728692-6-3 (alk. paper)
I. Johnston, Bill. II. Title.
PG7179.U45S5813 2004
891.8'538 – dc22   2003020335

Archipelago Books
www.archipelagobooks.org

Distributed by
Penguin Random House
www.penguinrandomhouse.com

Jacket art: *Luftschloss;* Oil, watercolor, gypsum on cardboard;
Kunstmuseum Bern, Hermann and Margritt Rupf Collection.
© 2003 Artists Rights Society (ARS), New York/VG Bild-Kunst, Bonn.

This publication has been funded by the Adam Mickiewicz Institute –
the © POLAND Translation Program

PRINTED IN THE UNITED STATES OF AMERICA

Dreams and Stones

THE TREE OF THE WORLD, LIKE EVERY OTHER TREE, at the beginning of the season of vegetation puts out tiny delicate golden leaves which with time acquire a dark green hue and a silvery sheen. Then they become yellow and red as if they were burning in a live flame and when they have burned their last they go brown and fall to earth ragged and full of holes, akin to pieces of paper turned to ash or rusted-through tin cans. From the first moments when the greenery is freshest and the greatest number of birds are singing amongst the branches a damp and dark countertree is growing into the depths of the earth, infested with vermin. The underground trunk is an extension of the trunk above ground; every bough is connected by an invisible water duct to a counterbough oppressed by tons of earth.

As the season of vegetation draws to a close the tree of the world is laden with fruit. The fruit ripens, falls and rots. In each fruit there is a seed and in that seed the germ of the tree and the countertree, crown and root. All the future seasons of vegetation await their turn in the seeds, in the germs, in the germs of the germs. The fruit belongs to the tree but contains within itself a whole future tree along with the fruit that will grow upon it.

The cities that ripen on the tree of the world are enclosed in shape like apples. Each is the same: Every one is different. An embodiment of a singular possibility from the register of the possible is the very name written above the railroad platforms. One river – a second is unnecessary – fixes its course definitively once and for all. One list of streets, one zoological garden. The inhabitants know by heart the colors of the clouds and of the plaster. Whatever comes to be can no longer be any different. When one thing is given to them another must be taken away. Every glance of theirs is accompanied by an awareness of loss. Crossing the city, they keep feverishly imagining what could yet be. If for instance the river flows broad and sluggish, passing shoals of sand, sooner or later they will create the other river, which was not given to them, deep and rapid, with steep banks overgrown with weeds. And so when the city germinates, when it ripens and when it rots, it contains within itself all possibilities at once, and the entire plan of the world. It is part and whole, infinitude and a godforsaken backwater, a particle in the world and at the same time an abyss into which the world vanishes – tiny as a fly in the ointment. For the rule that governs larger and smaller wholes declares that the small is contained in the large and the large in the small. And it is only thanks to this that the world fitted into itself. And it is only in this way that it can endure. Because otherwise it would have nowhere to go.

When the tree of life burned in a live flame and its leaves turned to ash and fell from its branches it was not long before something began to sprout from a stray seed. Why did it happen at that particular time, why in that place and why in that way? It was determined by the unrepeatable properties of the season, by the quality of the soil and by the winds. It could not have been otherwise. There began to grow simultaneously public buildings and residential buildings, large, medium-sized and smallish, soaring or squat, sumptuous or plain. They grew out from under the earth and climbed upward encased in wooden scaffolding in clouds of lime dust amid confusion and uproar with the creaking of wheelbarrows, the scrape of trowels, sudden warning shouts and the dull thud of falling bricks.

No one knows where the power came from that set all this in motion and caused the walls to thrust upward. Nor how many spadefuls of earth had to be dug out for a single excavation to appear. Nor how much toil is needed before walls appear over the rim of the excavation, to say nothing whatsoever of roofs, window frames or plaster. The destiny of the seed is to swell and sprout; the power that lies within it serves that purpose alone. It is this power that draws the sand and lime into the circulation of substances necessary for the walls to rise. The mounds of loamy soil required faith, like the water that awakens life. Faith filled the hearts of those transporting cement and passing bricks. The mounds of earth absorbed as much of it as they could. At that time there was no shortage of faith, as opposed to knowledge, of which it seems there was as yet little. For only a person who did not know the dimensions of the task that had been undertaken could dig like this without fear in the face of the avalanche of further obligations that would inevitably be unleashed. There was only one way it could have been stopped: by filling in the excavations as quickly as possible so that there was nothing left to complete.

Not one doubt clouded their minds; the bricklayers believed in the vertical and the horizontal and also in mortar. And they believed firmly that everything the mind creates (even safety pins, even rosin) ought to exist in the world. No one doubted that in a city there should be streets and so also water carts to sprinkle the streets on hot days when they get dusty. And trams and trucks that would drive day and night from one suburb to another and back again. That it was necessary to create chauffeurs, mechanics, drivers and ticket collectors, nurses and police officers.

In order to summon this whole throng to life it was enough to sew denim overalls, white aprons with stiff caps and uniforms of gray woolen cloth. But machines were required to produce the yarn and to stitch the clothes and also needles, tailors' shears and so on. The world had barely appeared yet already everything was needed, and immediately too. Necessary things and the tools essential in their manufacture, without distinction, preferably at the same time. And raw materials: steel, coal, kerosene, paper and ink, not forgetting the yellow oil paint for painting the walls in waiting rooms.

Such a great accumulation of urgent needs engendered frenetic haste, tension and uncertainty. For what ought to come first, the lathe or the screw for it, the cast iron or the great furnace, the egg or the hen? The world had only just emerged from its primordial chaos when it found itself at once faced with a colossal task fit for the hands of giants, a task as vast as the world itself and laborious as the threading of a needle; a job whose boundlessness swallowed without a trace the first spadefuls of earth removed from where the foundations of future factories were to be laid.

Ebonite telephones were produced, into which people had to shout at the top of their lungs, covering one ear with a hand; and cardboard folders tied with ribbons; great black typewriters; indelible pencils; and many other things. There appeared massive inkstands made of thick glass, wooden blotters lined with blotting paper that bore navy blue stains, mounts for pen nibs and the nibs themselves. The furniture smelled of fresh polish. The dark red of signs blossomed on the walls, proclaiming the advent of times of granite and sandstone on slabs that weighed two tons apiece: the beginning of the era of immense blocks of gray marble and all other durable building materials, grand in nature, as if they had been created for the decoration of monumental façades and interiors. The core of the city however was a round billion of red bricks, more real than anything else at all. Each of them had passed through many hands and all disappeared beneath the plaster and the sandstone facing. Coarse fragments remained which children would play with in the courtyards for a long time to come.

In those happy times all future days seemed altogether fresh and tidily arranged, like young leaves that have not yet emerged from the bud. Every boy would become a pilot and every little girl a schoolteacher. And in the school cloakrooms leather flying caps hung in anticipation, while on every scrap of concrete there appeared classrooms crookedly outlined in white chalk. Everything was possible. The world looked orderly, the foundations were deep, the walls thick, the pipes brand new. At the thought of "the world" what came to mind was above all that which can be touched: walls and pipes, loose sand, soft clay, cold water, rough fragments of red brick, lime dust. And that which can only be observed from afar, but which always returns to its place at the proper time of the day and year: the sun and the stars in the sky, the flag fluttering in the breeze. And also that which is always there and about which one never thinks: the air in one's lungs, the earth underfoot. It was trodden confidently, in certainty that it truly existed.

The growth of a city in many respects resembles the growth of a tree. Two intersecting streets laid out in the beginning sprout ever more numerous cross-streets, which in time send out their own and so on without end. Successive intersections arise; soft surfaces are paved over; a network of water pipes expands, hidden beneath the ground. A tree grows through the vitality of the seed and the juices drawn from the earth but the shape and density of the crown depend on the person who trims the branches with pruning shears. A city too grows through power and faith. But its layout quite evidently depends on the way the foundations are set down. Thus in analyzing the arrangement of the streets it is possible to discern the will and the beliefs that have left their stamp on it.

The arrangement of the streets in turn was devised in such a way as to thwart chance occurrences and to avert convoluted thoughts. Since life is from a certain perspective only a replication of urban design, order in the city compels order in the mind. The creators of the plan, whoever they were, achieved their purpose though they did not trust in architecture and scorned the tricks of city planning. No detail was overlooked in their decisions; they presented their demands in raised voices and took complications in their stride, hammering their fists upon the table. They did not have to adapt their intentions to fit the rules of an art foreign to them. The defiant simplicity of their treatments indicates that in fact they were proud of this. They knew nothing of logarithms but they understood that complexity is a cause of error. They sought a principle of construction that would determine the form of the city conclusively and comprehensively and would always protect it from the destructive influence of ambiguity.

Here it must be explained categorically that the guiding principle of a city can be the right angle, the meander or the star. It is this that shapes the course of events which will play out in the city from the very beginning of its existence: the meetings, the collisions, the coincidences. To say nothing of the circulation of the clouds. From the blueprint emerge the exigencies of life, from the examples in textbooks come the laws of physics, never the other way around.

For example a city of right angles is such that the location of one thing in relation to another signifies no more than distance and direction. Space cannot absorb or convey any substance beyond the purely practical, superficial, and indifferent. Every corner is equally important. Monuments are merely figures of stone besoiled by pigeons. The value of land, regulated by supply and demand, can easily be expressed in currency. The vacillations of stock prices are subject to no one's will. There exists no force capable of tipping the equally laden scales. Nothing that would ensure the appearance of only heads or only tails on coins spun in the air. Nothing that would make every card drawn from the pack turn out to be the ace of hearts or alternately the two of spades. Through a point that does not lie on a straight line it is only ever possible to draw one straight line parallel to the first. For this reason even justice here is as pedantic as geometry, devoid of inspiration or panache, predictable.

The principle of the meander turns streets into a chaotic labyrinth, creating countless numbers of figures of various shapes on top of each other and permeating one another, any of which may turn out to be part of a larger whole. A city that conforms to the principle of the meander will prove to be filled with tempting or terrifying possibilities, appetizing or nauseating leftovers, enticing or repulsive smells, and mingled sounds: shop sign against shop sign, rickshaw on rickshaw, without a single centimeter of free space. From every square a variety of streets leads to the next square, making the inhabitants' heads spin and their eyes flit about in every direction, their minds cluttered with the perpetual weighing of alternatives. Everything turns out to be relative, while the observation of relations of consequence, the attribution of effects to causes, the laying down of parallel lines, and the dispensation of justice are not possible at all.

Only the inhabitants of a city built according to the design of the star are never faced with the necessity of choice. They are obliged to move around in straight lines, yet in a certain sense all straight lines there are parallel. In every place only one appropriate road meets the eye. And so the calm pedestrians look directly ahead, which gives them an expression of infinite patience. The main streets there lead radially to the most important point, which marks the true center. In it is situated the heart of the city. From here the whole city is clearly visible; in the twinkling of an eye one can see right through it along with all its interiors, even its telephone wells, its storm drains and its rows of cellars. It contains within itself a lasting record of the order of the world to which it belongs and an invaluable ready outline of the values that will be assigned to the things it contains. The gravitational force of the objects placed in the scales will depend not only on their mass but above all on their estimated worth. Thanks to the shrewdness of these estimations it will transpire that things that have not occurred will often be more deserving of praise or scorn than those that have actually taken place.

On clean drafting paper it is easiest to draw rectangles. Thanks to the mechanical properties of draftsmen's instruments, they multiply on its surface of their own accord, leaving no room for other shapes. Stars, on the other hand, originate in the mind. There, far from earth, this breeding ground of ants and worms, they glitter all at once, and their irrepressible rays slice through the darkness. But no one knows where the meander comes from; it is foreign to sober reason that aids the movements of set squares, and foreign, too, to luminous imaginings. Its twisting form is evidence of the resistance presented to the essence of the meander by the set square and rule and also by the thought guiding the pencil. The star's ray bends in the field of attraction of every rectangle and having broken free seeks its straight path anew – and then again and once more, always without success. The intricacy of the drawing demonstrates that the design of the star, woven from dreams, is incongruent with the worldly design of right angles arising from lines drafted on paper. But between the forces of the rectangle and the star a state of equilibrium may emerge and be sustained amid the meanders of ideology and dry calculation.

And what about the intention of putting down lines? Why did the draftsmen begin to draw them instead of waiting for them to appear by themselves on the surface of the paper or even in space? In ordering the lines to be drawn the builders revealed their belief in one of the possible truths that could be thought, on a basis that would always remain a matter of faith since it was by nature unverifiable. Though it remains a supposition it is not hard to interpret. It proclaims that it is not the power of germinating seeds and not the pressure of juices circulating between the roots and the crown that give the world life, but that it is set in motion by motors, gears, and cogs, devices that keep the sun and stars rotating, pull the clouds across the horizon and drive water along the bed of the river. The clarity and simplicity of this notion may prove salutary. They will make it possible to dismantle, repair and reinstall every broken component – so long as the world is composed only of separate and removable parts and any process can be corrected independently of all the others without worrying that the whole will become imbalanced. Put another way, cities based on stars and cities based on right angles are superior to cities based on meanders, so long as the world is a machine.

The builders had the privilege of certainty. They knew truths that were not subject to doubt. But they kept them to themselves. Where now can one find the certainty that the world is a machine since in so many respects it resembles a tree? Like the tree with its countertree, so each object in the world is linked to its counterobject and all that is visible is connected with something invisible. Between the visible and the invisible parts of the tree there is a perpetual flow of juices from the roots to the leaves. As they turn yellow and fall off, the leaves quit the heights of boughs and return where their substance came from – the roots. They become dark and damp like the roots, they mingle with earth and water and when invisible they are drawn within them. Despite the life-giving flow of juices the separation of the tree from the countertree is technically feasible. The builders cut down trees successfully. Though here it should be noted that during this operation life slips away from both parts. The same happens with anything else: After the visible part is separated from the invisible part everything withers and shrivels up. Not everything, say some, and they also know a thing or two. But what survives will turn out to be part of a theatrical set or a dream.

It is hard to work when it is unclear which truth should be adhered to. When we think of the world as a tree we see a tree, when we think of it as a machine it is a machine. In both cases observations corroborate one's assumptions, in both cases everything falls into place. Things are not provided with any telltale sign; there is no maxim to which one can appeal. Anyone who says, "it is a tree," will immediately think of a machine; whoever says, "it is a machine," will think at once of a tree. For this reason the expressions "it is a tree" and "it is not a tree" in essence mean the same thing. Would it not be better if the creators of the project were right? They treated the world as if it were a machine and were prepared at any moment to remove and repair whatever needed it. And thanks to the certainty that was their lot, separating objects from counterobjects turned out to be childishly simple. For a machine contains nothing that can be destroyed during the act of separation. It is inanimate by assumption and from the beginning and no one expects things to be otherwise. After the casing is removed the parts can be seen. There is no secret here, nothing elusive, nothing that cannot be touched. Even the rules governing the breakdown of parts are utterly plain. It is clear that they are associated with dust and water vapor finding their way into the mechanism. If the world is a machine then the separation of object from counterobject must begin with the sealing up of the casing. And from the construction of a vault that will rest on solid ground. By this means the upper and lower waters will be parted and from that moment it will be obvious what is the top and what is the bottom, what is order and permanence and what is chaos and change. And only then will it be possible to distinguish night from day.

A properly sealed casing will protect the world from dust and vapor coming from the outside. However, the solving of one problem opens the door to further complications. Cooling apparatuses need to be installed to prevent the mechanism from overheating. The more auxiliary devices there are the more dust and vapor there is on the inside, released by friction and by differences in temperature. The final separation of movement from friction, warmth from cold and good from evil requires only an installation to remove vapor, dust and dirt beyond the dome of the sky directly into the churning waters that swirl on the other side of the vault. Thus the difficulty of separating the city from the countercity comes down to powering all the essential devices. In accordance with the conception of the project's creators a safe dry space beneath the vault requires effective seals and large power stations.

The city spread out on the draftsman's blueprint had something festive about it. It had been designed with the thought of sunny days and no one even knew what it would look like in rainy weather. The sidewalks with their evenly laid-out flags recalled squared paper or the other way round: The square-patterned paper copied the stones of the sidewalk. There was no space for kitchen refuse lying about near trash cans. On one of the streets there was a kindergarten, on another bricklayers walked along in pants stained with lime while on a third a band played with gleaming trumpets. Care was taken that the sun should shine both on the bricklayers and on the kindergarten although – it goes without saying – it shone most handsomely of all on the trumpets.

All this could also be seen in the photographs appearing in the daily press. There bricklayers with their caps pulled down over their brows saw the deliberation of a bricklayer over a game of drafts on Saturday after work, the confidence of a bricklayer writing a compound fraction on the blackboard at night school, the pride of a bricklayer showing a new building to a trim-looking nurse. For newspapers were among the first things that appeared in the world, even, it seemed, before the creation of printing presses.

The news photos came into contact with our world through the surface of the paper yet they had their own depth in which pasteboard suitcases, kept under bunk beds in twenty-person dormitories, were filled not with loops of sausage and not with fustian long johns but with books about the lives of bricklayers. For in that world what could be more interesting for a bricklayer than the life of a bricklayer, the work of a bricklayer, the thoughts of a bricklayer? The same applied to turners, foundrymen, fitters, and all the other people who lived happily in the other world beneath the surface of the paper.

The original plan of the city consisted of a drawing of many symmetrically arranged square shapes linked harmoniously to a great central rosette. It should be stated that the acoustics were excellent. A garland of megaphones arrayed around the base of the central building sufficed to bring sound to every street. The palace erected in the center of the rosette was filled with marble and mirrors. From ceilings so high they were scarcely visible and seemed always to be shrouded in mist there hung crystal chandeliers outspread like fountains. Of the ten thousand double doors at least half were locked from the very beginning since they were needed not for access but for symmetry. As the latter concept so closely expressed the notion of the mechanical equilibrium of the world, it was elevated to the status of guiding principle in the project. In the meantime the keys to the doors had been mixed up and lost from the start. Every bricklayer, machinist or foundryman who entered the interior would doff his herringbone cap and twist it in his hands, gazing about in admiration at the walls and ceilings, and would retire at once to the exit, having glanced by accident into a mirror in its gilt frame.

The mirrors were little smaller than the walls on which they hung, one opposite another, duplicating their reflections into infinity. Kilometers of tiled floors retreated into the distance of mirrored spaces, into the boundless world that is separated from ours by the surface of the glass. An endless number of cleaning women had to work without a break in all the mirrors, polishing the floors from morning till evening all through the month; before they finished their work, it was time to start over again.

From the ground level, elevators shot up like speeding bullets to the highest floor; they were operated by female attendants with silver buttons who sat on gold-colored stools. From the dizzy heights the tramcars below looked like matchboxes and the people like ants, while dogs and pigeons could not be seen at all. That world, in which everything was so small, bordered on the highest floors through the panes of windows that were always closed, and it was only from there that it was visible. It was not easy to reach the miniature square that the miniature tramcar was passing. One first had to break the window, lean outside, hear the whistle of the wind and ask for the last time if this was truly what one desired. For in that world, where everything was small, all one could do was die.

The edifice, which reached as high as the clouds, on certain frosty days resembled a glass mountain crowned by a needle with an icy sheen. On foggy days passersby would be startled when it loomed unexpectedly out of the whiteness and revealed itself for a moment, very close, immense, immense, and then just as suddenly disappeared. Though efforts were made to prevent other buildings from concealing it, due to the changeability of the weather and the light it could not always be in plain view. But it was this building that was the heart of the city. In the evening it grew completely deserted and was locked up, in this way isolating the heart from the rest of the organism. It may be that at night the city did not require a heart. Because what would a heart be, in the machinery of the city, if not its principal pump and central valve, a place where the pressure of the flow of what is necessary and what is unnecessary is regulated? It would seem that at night, when the city slept, there was no flow and all movement ceased.

At the moment when the centrally located palace was locked up shoals of fifteen-watt lightbulbs could be observed from its heights. By their wan light it would have been possible to see, all set out carefully as in a doll's house, dressers painted with oil paints, grayish laundry drying on clotheslines strung from the ceiling, rust-colored patches of damp on the walls, packages wrapped in greasy paper and jars of pickled cucumbers hidden from the sight of the tenants across the way, behind lace curtains fastened with tacks to the lower sections of the windows. Above all one would have seen, through billows of steam rising from kettles, unshaven men in undershirts and women in dressing gowns. Who were these people and where had they come from? If someone had looked closely they might have recognized them. But the top floor, from which such an extensive and curious sight was to be observed, remained unoccupied.

The builders did not live there. They were above the everyday; they had no need of kettles, dressers or lace curtains and had no use for clotheslines or for jars of pickled cucumbers. In all probability they lived nowhere. Or rather they lived everywhere, but only in the way that music lives in a concert hall, filling the entire space with its existence. It was they who were lit up in the electric lightbulbs, who fluttered in pennants, and who ticked inside clocks. It was they who, hanging on the walls and looking down keenly through framed glass, thrust the countercity from the city with the power of their gaze. Beneath their eyes cleaning women cleaned, clerks filed documents and mechanics scrubbed and oiled machines. It was precisely for this that the mechanics, clerks, cleaners and all the others rose from their beds every day and donned their assigned outfits. It was for this that the seamstresses sewed, and the bakers baked rolls for them; for this the tram drivers drove their trams, and the bricklayers constructed buildings for them. All the while the children of all these people learned in kindergarten to tie and untie their shoelaces and ate their porridge and milk, waving their spoons about, in order to grow up without delay and reinforce the ranks of those who made sure order was maintained.

Cleaning and repairing, repairing and cleaning, laborious efforts to keep the chaos on the outside, the daily repulsing of the countercity – all this utterly filled the lives of the inhabitants, even though they themselves might imagine they were doing something else, earning money to live on or trying to overcome the hardships of life. And even if the city was equipped with some kinds of special devices to remove what was unnecessary, they had no interest in this, confident that the appropriate office would take care of them.

It was for this race of people with straightforward, cheerful minds that the beautiful streets, squares and gardens were meant; for them were the floors of marble and sandstone and even the mirrors in their gilded frames. It was for them that those times were opened wide toward the broad expanses of the future, toward its boundless plateaus where there rose higher and higher chimneys and further on chimneys higher than the highest ones and others even higher; it seemed that in the future there would be no limit to the height of chimneys. It was precisely the beauty of chimneys that was associated with the captivating charm of the future, that distant realm extending always a little up and to the left-hand side, toward which rose the hopeful gaze of the bricklayer and the steelworker on posters tacked up on the fences around the building sites.

In the beginning the reserves of faith and strength seemed as inexhaustible as the deposits of coal. These reserves, like the coal, lay somewhere down below, underneath the feet of steelworker and bricklayer – feet planted widely as a sign of conviction. Thus, simply through the feet's contact with the ground faith and strength filled the hearts of the simple, brave people as they stared at that place up there to the left.

The builders gave unstintingly of hands, with thousands of them at their disposal. It may be that they yielded to the temptation to create beauty as well as order, to impose enchantment alongside obedience. Despite the enormous labors required to set the world in motion and to maintain its order painstaking ornamental work was undertaken. Fanciful grates and gutters were made, though beauty served no practical purpose. Thanks to the overabundance of faith and strength, façades were adorned with attics and bas-reliefs, and statues appeared in the recesses of walls. These figures of stone were clad in stone aprons, stone shirts with rolled-up sleeves and stone pants. Their stance was imperturbable; they had protruding eyes without pupils and held a bricklayer's trowel or carried a pickax over their shoulder. They were a hard-handed race who wore clothes sewn by stone seamstresses and ate loaves of stone; the ablest of the master craftsmen who at the beginning of the world, out of bricks, sheet metal and plaster created all the wonders of that world. Inside their stone pockets were stone documents with a photograph and a stamp from the residence office, stone certificates and stone letters of recommendation. But these cannot be seen, because for us stones have only a surface. The solid interior of the stone belongs to another world: a world in which unity of substance prevails. Ligaments and muscles are as hard as shirt and apron. There is no boundary between the heart and the document in the breast pocket; none between head and cap or between hand and tool.

The unimaginable homogeneity of the stone was an object of wonder, a matchless model and example. For each of the bricklayers made of stone there were dozens of living ones, shock workers on the building sites, yet on whose hands blisters appeared from the handling of bricks and whose documents – while they themselves were beating records on the scaffolding – lay under lock and key in the manager's desk at the workers' hostel as security for the blankets they had borrowed from the storeroom; otherwise they could have taken the blankets with them, quitting their job without reason. Fate had presented these people with tasks that were great and important or petty and inconsequential. For each exalted one there were a hundred others imitating every movement of his hands, and a thousand more who had only once ever had the opportunity to see him from a distance, craning their necks as they stood in the crowd.

So that the labor should not be forgotten, and its goal properly understood by the benign sea of heads covered in herringbone caps, a watch was awarded to the hand that laid the first hundred bricks, the one that poured the first steel, and the one that set the first lathe in motion. Photographs were taken of front teeth bared in a smile and tight-fitting jackets decorated with sashes that bore an appropriate inscription. And beneath the jackets was the calm, even, synchronized beating of dark red hearts that were not prone to arrhythmia or pain or even fatigue and kept on pumping blood to the bulging blue veins on work-worn hands. This was how the age of commemorative watches began and also the age of commemorative teapots and irons, an age of ever new inscriptions on sashes, ever new faces in photographs and challenge trophies which were constantly being given and taken away, whereas the cut of the jackets, the rhythm of the hearts and the shape of veins in the hands did not change in the slightest. At its rapturous peak this age was ablaze with crimson plush and gilding, instinct with the trembling of countless rows of seats facing a stage enfolded in draperies and bearing a magnificent presidial table. There resounded torrents of speeches and especially thunderous cascades of applause filling the concert halls in place of music, which none of them needed any longer, even operettas. The echo of shoes creaking in the hallways, the whispers, the coughs and especially the clatter of tin spoons in the snack bar – all this disappeared without a trace in the background.

At that time the machinery of the world worked smoothly, without grinding noises or surprises, like the machinery of a stage that enables practiced hands to move the sky along with the stars and the sun and to turn the earth, flat as a plate, with the aid of a special crank. In this time of the world's infancy, with the necessary effort the impossible also turned out to be achievable.

In the meantime the city blossomed moment by moment. On the blueprints colonnades reached to the fourth and fifth floors; golden fountains played in the squares while hanging gardens extended overhead and there flew past helicopters which were used by the municipal transit authorities and for which landing pads had been planned on rooftops as big as city squares; while underground, hovercraft moved quietly along barely touching their rails. And trams, trams and more trams ran from dawn till midnight and from one end of the city to the other and back again.

Imperceptibly the network of tram cables grew beyond all measure. The hanging gardens receded before them. Ground waters appeared whose complex system necessitated changes in the subterranean installations connected with the hovercraft traffic; it suddenly transpired that lines drawn on drafting paper could be threatened by water flowing somewhere beneath the earth. In this way, in the city emerging within the plans modifications appeared that could not have been predicted and that curbed the momentum of the city growing in space. Nevertheless the chimneys sprang upward without hindrance and were indeed ever taller and more splendid. They were constantly being observed and also photographed and filmed. They appeared in the posters stuck on fences around each new building site, where, stern and black, resembling exclamation points, they served as a background to vivid red letters. Along with the chimneys there rose lofty slag heaps, silos containing cement, and warehouses. Yet at times it seemed that all this was not enough and that the movement should be even faster, the exclamation point even more emphatic.

Time was barely able to keep up with the rapidity of thought. The days were counted and planned out many years in advance and if these calculations contained any errors, they never involved a surplus. It could be said that the days were used up before they arrived, like anticipated assets against which debts have already been incurred. Time, like electricity, was a good that had a specific value and purpose. Thus everything humanly possible was done to accelerate its passage. It is even likely that use was made of certain possibilities for improving the efficiency of astronomical phenomena. There came a time when the city hurtled round like a carousel; scarcely had it emerged from dawn than it already sank into darkness and with it its factories and steel mills and its plumes of sparks and its smoke filled with fumes and sulfur, which turned black as pitch in the red light of the rising and setting sun. While successive tons of new steel were being forged the old steel was wearing out and rotting upon the earth, beneath the earth and in the air. Newly manufactured paper was delivered immediately to the printing presses, where it was used to print newspapers that the very same day ended up in the trash.

The trams had barely pulled in to the depot before they had to set out on their routes again; the street lamps had scarcely gone out when they had to come on once more; milk bottles and bowls of porridge were perpetually being filled and emptied, while yesterday's children were already putting on and taking off hats, brassieres and neckties. Men were constantly shaving; their stubble would grow back in the blink of an eye between one morning and the next. Bed sheets appeared and disappeared on foldaway sofa beds with no more than a flash of white; one after another, tanks of gasoline, kerosene and gas were emptied in the thousands and tens of thousands. There was no hope that the speeding cycle of past and future tasks would finally attain its goal – a sufficiency of the paper, steel and other substances the city voraciously demanded – that it would finally be sated and things would be able to slow down.

In this mad rush no one looked carefully enough to also notice what was in the background. Thought was led by appearances and it was hard to recognize the thing that one's eye lighted upon. In this way all the worlds were mixed together: the world that bordered on this one through the surface of newspaper photographs with its own depth, the world that opened up in mirrors and the world that was visible from the highest floors in which people were as tiny as little toys. Only the world that unfolded inside the stones and could not be seen retained its frontiers.

The momentum of the city was in certain respects becoming onerous. From the incessant clicking of switches the instrument panels wore out; for this reason it was eventually decided not to turn the lights out at all, not to turn the machines off and not to go to bed. The uninterrupted work of factories and power plants in turn made it possible to accelerate the passage of time even more; this opportunity was not passed over. The present shot by at a rate of twenty-four frames per second; at the same speed, amid a low hum, images of the factories and power plants were wound onto massive spools right until movement finally began to cease and against a dark background there appeared a white inscription: THE END.

For everything that has a beginning also has an end. The tape must be of the right length so it can be wound onto the spool and after being shown it can be put away in its flat metal can. If only for this reason time limits both the filming and the projection. The bulb of the projector can shine for a specified number of hours, rather less than more; it was installed in the projector after the previous bulb burned out and in time it too will burn out. What happens to the factories and power plants after the projector is switched off? They are dispersed. A certain aspect of them finds its way into the flat metal can; another aspect remains beneath the eyelids of the moviegoers standing up from their seats. Yet another is expressed in the cable that joins the projector to the electrical outlet and through it to the entire machinery of the world, which for a certain period did indeed work quickly and efficiently and then – it was unclear when – began to slow down. For momentum too has a beginning and an end.

The laws of nature on which the plans for development were at one time based declared that what grows quickly will grow even more quickly, that explosion rules out implosion and that motionlessness is foreign to motion. The calculations that arose from these laws initially produced satisfactory approximations. They continued to be applied for some time, errors being dismissed with a shrug of the shoulders, until it became evident that the approximations being used had ceased to be adequate. For they failed to make adjustments for the wheel of fortune, for the unstable course of the affairs of this world, for the sudden unforeseen vagaries of fate. They did not make allowance for the chance obstacle that will stop an inscrutable thought in flight. They knew nothing of the vibrations that would cause the ever more powerfully thundering megaphones to fall apart. The greater the acceleration a speeding locomotive has the sooner it must begin to brake, otherwise disaster will ensue. A crane that bears record loads will eventually collapse under the excessive burden. Fatigue of the materials, and also arrhythmia and pain, will suddenly manifest themselves in advanced stages. The curve of growth sooner or later will reach the edge of the chart and be suspended in the air.

The consciousness of this state of things emerged gradually and did not shake the foundations of the city. Amazement was spread over a long time, during which some began to have their suspicions and others refused to hear anything about it. Another generalization slowly began to spread which proclaimed that what was large would become small and not larger still, what was full would be empty and what grew tall would sink beneath the earth. In practice the new formula produced approximations that were at least as good as before, if not better; since it was easier it quietly displaced the old one, even though it irritated many. Whoever began to apply it was liberated from pathos, and on their lips appeared an ironic half-smile like a secret stamp. Its ever more numerous adherents, laboring without enthusiasm, accomplished neither more nor less than previously, when they had given their all, working their fingers to the bone. The discovery that a fiasco does not require sacrifices brought relief.

Should the making of adjustments for the fatigue of materials be condemned as a sign of faintheartedness? Can a conciliatory attitude toward their natural tendency to decay and rust be labeled cynicism? Gearwheels wear down and convert ever greater amounts of energy into ever fewer revolutions. They once were new but now are old, used up, for the trash heap. And the cogs of the world also turned more slowly than before, both from the worn gears and because of the defective power source. The skies with their stars and sun revolved more slowly and even the clouds moved less rapidly, drawn sluggishly on invisible strings by a dilapidated motor.

The greediest consumers of energy were the installations that sorted order from chaos, those that separated the city from the countercity. It was these installations that would grind to a halt at every break in the power supply, threatening an emergency of catastrophic proportions. For everything depended on these devices just as a steamship with a leaky hull depends on efficient pumps to keep it afloat on the ocean. It is possible that without them the city would have ceased to exist in an instant, submerged by the turbulent waves of the countercity. Rather let the tramcars stand idle, it was decided, and they stood for hours on end, all in a line, abandoned. For a long time it was still possible to ensure a continuous supply of power to the special mechanisms at the cost of the production lines and the street lights.

It transpired that the greatest resistance to breakdown was presented by clocks and watches, which did not require a constant power source. It was enough for someone to remember to wind them up once a day. But the speed of the hands no longer matched the present time. Each revolution of the minute hand around the dial corresponded with fewer revolutions of the gears or cylinders in the machines. The difference was not great but it was clear and tangible. For instance the lathes which had been the pride of the times of growth and development: As things slowed down, they began to produce many defective parts which made assembly difficult and held up production. The operators of the machines were glad of this. It turned out that the inhabitants of the city preferred resting to working. Each minute contained fewer movements of human hands than previously.

The day's work was too short for all the labors associated with maintaining order in the world: vacuuming, polishing floors, mending door handles, washing windows. The inhabitants of the city did not have time to eat dinner before sundown. They set aside their spring cleaning till summer was almost over, the leaves were turning yellow and snow was beginning to fall. They turned away from the growing backlog of jobs. What had been neglected always seemed impossible to make up, the vast amounts of work deprived them of hope, and no one wished even to remove their hands from their pockets. They smoked without taking the cigarette out of their mouths and tossed the butts underfoot. In the newspapers they read only the headlines. They took shortcuts by trampling over flower-beds and made no effort to save electricity. In kitchens beneath washing lines hung with threadbare laundry they scoffed at the naive labor of floor polishing, at marches played on golden trumpets and at lathes, great furnaces and even waiting rooms painted with yellow oil paint. In case of need worn parquet could be replaced with linoleum, a window pane with a sheet of plywood and a broken lampshade with newspaper. No one now looked for the right lampshade or a window pane of the appropriate dimensions, since the inhabitants of the city began to realize that any thing could be replaced with some other thing just as any word could be replaced with another word of the same or – equally well – of the opposite meaning. They no longer cared about things and even less about words; they sought only oblivion.

They defended themselves as best they could from the rapacious city, that immense leech sucking all their strength out of them. They moved slowly like sick people and were sparing in their gestures. Whatever they had to do they wondered whether it might be possible not to bother. It was for this reason that they even jumped out of the way of tramcars too late. Hope, said to be the mother of fools, abandoned the city. In its absence pity also went missing. People laughed at those who were swindled and those who were run over when the light was green. They lorded over the weak and kowtowed to the powerful. They got drunk, seduced women and abandoned them, embezzled money, informed on one other and wept.

No one knew if the perfection of the city was meant to be passed on to its inhabitants or whether on the contrary it was originally hoped that the inhabitants would already be perfect. Those whose lot it was to live there would shout angrily that a person would have to be a saint to even put up with the place.

Or they would ask whether frailty was a defect of the race or rather was the consequence of an error in urban planning. They cast doubt on the intentions of those who had created the project. They asked whom the palace had been built for that stood empty at night with its spire reaching up to the clouds. They laughed at the belief that anyone could manage without cupboards and they expressed the suspicion, which quite independently suggested itself, that the creators of the project had a need for even more magnificent interiors and concealed them somewhere as deep as the spire was high.

At kitchen tables, over cups of tea growing cold they conjectured that they were not the ones for whom the city was built. They themselves knew that everything in them was too soft and too fragile, that their will bent too easily while their desires ran first one way and then the other without rhyme or reason. Their hands barely matched the handles of their tools; their hearts were utterly isolated from the rest of the world by a cage of ribs and an integument of skin. There was nothing here for them; all around they found strangeness.

Certain signs – such as the warm tone of voice of radio announcers as they recounted the course of mass celebrations – suggested that hope was still placed in them. That to them, local people, belonged the task of producing that perfect race untrammeled by doubt or fear of emptiness, the race that perhaps the city was waiting for. For them it was certainly not waiting: All those employed in the local factories and offices, recorded in the registration lists and in the ledgers of the registry office, exhausted by their hardships and their lust for comforts, suffered from problems of the stomach, liver and teeth and were tormented by shortness of breath. But despite all this the thought that their women were to give birth to children of another clay, different from their parents, was disagreeable to them.

From other signs – for example, sarcastic comments about the laziness of turners and fitters printed in the broadsheets of factories and pinned to the walls – the inhabitants of the city could conclude that they were an interim species that was to yield to another better than itself, which would appear once the city finally achieved perfection. These unpalatable speculations gave birth to troubling visions of having to move out. No one wanted to take their belongings and their children and leave that unloved place, the only one they had. Humiliated, they fell into an obstinate, angry silence. No one wanted the coming of children of stone or the appearance of new tribes. And everyone was more or less reconciled to what they already had.

There were also those from whom the inhabitants of the city could hear that it had been perfect for some time now – much too good for the drivers, fitters, nurses and bus conductors, cleaning ladies and their mechanic husbands who lived in it. All that riff-raff.

Quite unexpectedly refrigerators and washing machines appeared in the world, some of them broken from the very beginning. And also televisions in whose innards, through a glass screen people gazed in astonishment at a trembling, indistinct, black-and-white world the like of which no one had ever seen before. In the meantime more and more disorder was creeping into their lives. Over the years the city plan grew ever more complicated. The basic pattern of the star was effaced and little remained of the grand symmetry of the project, as if the world lacked the ideal of the mechanical equilibrium that was meant to be conveyed by the orderliness of the architectural treatments. With time the plan of the city included ever more irregular shapes lying across and upon one another in an inappropriate and disturbing way. Certain streets that previously had been broad and straight began to weave around, turning now one way, now the other with no sense of purpose or direction, seeming to forget the whole they were a part of and the angle at which they were supposed to intersect. In the place where a carousel had stood there would suddenly appear a plaza round as a plate, on whose wet asphalt cars would circle day and night. Where flocks of birds had passed through in the fall an overpass would arise which cars drove on one after another, heavy and ungainly, amidst clouds racing across the sky. The jammed viaduct released a spiral of them out of which – bursting through the iron guardrail – one by one they plummeted downward into puddles that shone with rainbowed patches of gasoline.

At times there were discrepancies between later plans and earlier ones. Successive projects were faced with an ever greater number of particular requirements and restrictions. The most recent were developed in multiple mutually exclusive versions, every one of which had some defect. An eight-story apartment building broke up the perspective of a street and blocked the view of the palace but a low shopping arcade in the same place was soon surrounded by crooked stalls that introduced a spirit of insubordination, disarray and truculence. An underground parking lot, spitting out dozens of automobiles per minute, could not be built in the proximity of the school, yet the school could not be closed down so as not to leave unsupervised the local children, who were in the habit of setting fire to trash bins and throwing stones at windows. Each of the projects was imperfect yet each had certain advantages; for this reason the limping whole spread out on the drafting boards needed all of them at once to avoid collapse. In this way space acquired a depth possessing qualities that could not be encompassed by the mind. Three dimensions are sometimes too many; what then of fifteen? Suffice it to say that park, viaduct and department store were able to occupy the same location in space without interfering with one another in the slightest, while their paths, escalators and lanes intersected without ever colliding.

Everything that happened on the draftsmen's desks was connected in a complex way with changes that took place in the city of bricks, where in the meantime there had appeared new bridges, new monuments and new chiming clocks. But the multiplicity of interpenetrating spaces and the accumulation of variants meant that none of these works had the panache of earlier ventures from the infancy of the world. Interiors became cramped, granite and sandstone ceased to be lavishly used, façades were no longer decorated with bas-reliefs which at some unknown moment had gone out of fashion. It should also be noted here that the new chimes rang somewhat out of tune and that their sound barely rose above the hubbub of the street.

It was easier and easier to see additional unplanned cities that had arisen no one knew when or how and that undermined the entirety with their hole-and-corner endurance. The police officer directing the traffic inhabits a city built of license plates to which are added car bodies, chassis, engines and turn signals. For the switchboard operator the metropolis of telephone receivers, enwrapped in cables, grows from the municipal telephone exchange as from a hidden rootstock. The drunkard's city is empty; it is composed only of undulating trails of light and hard edges rising up unhampered in space. Different still is the city of the dead person; it is entirely devoid of radiators, dank and dark; one cannot even ask for a cup of hot tea there and it is quite simply unlivable, especially at five o'clock in the morning, that coldest of hours.

Because of the existence of all these interpenetrating spaces a city becomes ever more confused, entangled, diffuse. It has to be simultaneously dark and light, crowded and deserted, noisy and soundless. And also, it must finally be admitted, it has to mean many things at once and mean nothing. Depending on the needs of the moment, its name could signify license plates, telephones, undulating trails of light, or anything else that in someone's eyes can form itself into a pattern called a city and that conceals the walls just as the beautiful and improbable glass of a kaleidoscope placed between the eye and the source of light takes the place of heaven and earth.

In this way the city misted over, lost its clear contours and became partly invisible. Yet even without seeing the city its inhabitants felt its existence distinctly enough. The rough walls of its buildings, the depth of stairwells bearing the dirty colors of oil paint, the unreliability of its elevators like cupboards suspended on steel cables in cavernous shafts, the scored interior walls, the spat-upon floors and broken bottles in corners. It was better not to see the never-washed windows in the factory halls or the machines whose lack of perfection was evident even when they stood idle. Their housings, covered in peeling paint, were thick and weighty, marked by the coarse angularity of the molds in which they had been made. Despite the uncomplicated nature of the casting every second one came out defective. Coal was not spared; enough of it was burned to turn the cast-iron shell back into red-hot pig iron. It was known that thinner castings would never work. Every part bore the stamp of its relationship with the hammer and the wrench; scratches testified to the lack of precision that weighed on these tools whose blind power was capable of breaking the resistance of rusted carbon-coated screws as thick as a finger.

The inhabitants of the city preferred not to broach openly the sensitive matter of the machines. They knew they had been built in a nostalgic adoration of perfection with a wish to amaze the world and that the substances out of which they had been made had always proved more unwieldy and intractable than that from which thoughts arise. The inquisitive and insolent operators of the machines encountered technical solutions introduced from elsewhere and compared their quality with that of the mythical original. In this city imitations never attained the level of their prototypes, whose brands were mentioned in a whisper with shining eyes, bringing the discussion to a close. The more magnificent they sounded the more contempt was felt for the local mechanisms of production that actually existed – the only ones that could be hooked up to the network and set in motion. While the mechanisms were still new people waited for them to be run in. This took place at some unknown point amongst successive breakdowns. Their gears jammed, their screws snapped and nuts fell into their cogwheels. The machinery of the city worked sluggishly amid earsplitting signs of damage, amid rattling and grinding. Here every object had its defects which were a part of its nature, perhaps the most important part, which needed only time to be revealed. That was why pipes had to become clogged and tanks had to leak. The more complex their construction the sooner they started to jam, fall apart and corrode.

At a certain time a large number of dark stars appeared in the sky of permanent stars which was suspended above the sky of clouds and below the sky of suns and moons. These were said to be merely ordinary stars that differed from others only in that for some reason they had died. And since they no longer shone they had become invisible. They were smashed to pieces by the helicopters of the municipal transit system which were roaming aimlessly beneath the vault of the sky without fuel, which they could not refill since there was nowhere to land: The landing pads on the rooftops had never been built and now they were overgrown with dense jungles of antennas.

The fragile lustrous substance that the stars were made of lost its transparent quality after the collisions and rained down on the city as a black dust. From it the plaster darkened. With time the buildings took on the same shade of gray as the cloudy sky and in this manner disappeared. As the problem of the power supply worsened successive stars were extinguished and ever greater quantities of black dust accumulated, falling like a shadow on sky and earth and obscuring every source of light, including the sun. The eyes of passersby skimmed over the tops of façades lost in the clouds. No one enjoyed any of the wonders of the city. The stone bricklayers in their stone clothing stood alone on heavy stone legs in the recesses of walls, needlessly wielding their pickaxes. With pigeons puffed up from the cold perched on their heads they endured, unnoticed, in the darkness of the street. The buildings, clouds and earth were all cloaked in the same hue and even the birds melted into the background. It was easier to see them in stamp albums, where at least they were not freezing.

No one knows where sorrow comes from in a city. It has no foundations; it is not built of bricks or screwed together from threaded pipes; it does not flow through electric cables nor is it brought by cargo trains. Sorrow drifts amongst the apartment buildings like a fine mist that the wind blows unevenly across the streets, squares and courtyards. There are long streets and short ones, there are broad ones and narrow ones. The gray of some bears a trace of ochre while others are bluish from the sidewalks to the roof tiles. Each of them has its own peculiar shade of sorrow. Those it has liberally coated and those it has marked with only a barely perceptible shadow run together, intersect and separate. Their length, breadth and angles of intersection influence the circulation of sorrow. Its volume and kind change every day in the city just like the weather. Here and there a small point of joy appears and a zone of joy begins to expand in wedges down streets enveloped in sorrow; its advance parts pass over the roofs of buildings like an atmospheric front. There are streets on which the flags of the sidewalk are loose and there is always a smell of cabbage and bacon while on Saturdays noise and music can be heard on every corner. Each Monday the place is filled with a dreary silence interrupted at infrequent moments by the slamming of doors and the sound of hoarse voices.

From a certain point of view sorrow might be regarded as an alternative form of enthusiasm which from the beginning was included in the plans for the city but – like everything in the world – proved not sufficiently durable and sooner or later had to turn into its opposite. Sorrow is what enthusiasm becomes when its explosion passes its highest point, after which implosion inevitably follows.

These were the discoveries of the inhabitants as they sought new rules in feverish desperation. For without rules life is lived in an intolerable uncertainty. Rules too are of little help. They do not enable one to touch either enthusiasm or sorrow, much less the causes of their appearance and disappearance. Little can be encompassed with the gaze – no more than a street corner or one side of a square, sometimes a sign over a store or a lace curtain in a window. Thoughts and imaginings, unlike walls, can be seen without opening one's eyes. This entire city standing here below on earth and covered with the dome of heaven is suspended in another vaster space where the names of all things and states arise and circulate and out of which thoughts emerge. Even the blind tapping the sidewalks with their white canes, their gaze fixed on the inside of their heads, never cease to be aware of the fact that something is rising or subsiding in that abyss.

Beneath the vaults of skulls there extend boundless expanses where no human has set foot and which contain things that are in plain view yet cannot be touched. Whereas that which is tangible endures in places trodden by feet yet closed to thoughts. The stone bricklayers will not see anything beyond what is seen by any brick or roof tile, though they stare untiringly without blinking day and night. Everything around them has its place yet nothing has a name. The city trodden by feet and the city in which thoughts swirl adjoin each other at the lens of the eye, by which they are scrupulously separated. Even the blind see what is most important: limitless darkness like the night sky, in which the constellations of the names of all things are scattered, shining and dying like stars.

This vast expanse is curved in such a curious way that everything that can be thought is always situated inside it. It can be crossed without the slightest effort; there is no need even to open one's eyes, for everyone knows what a telephone booth looks like, a bus or an opera house. It is woven from that which one knows without looking. And even if it never existed the telephone booth will always be found on the right corner exactly at the moment the bus pulls up at the stop in front of the opera house. It is enough to utter the appropriate word in order to summon up in an instant all the corners of that incorporeal city, all the signs above the stores and also all the bus stops – including those that exist only in someone's mistaken memory – and all the telephone booths, at every hour of the day and night, in rain, frost and swelter. All the buildings and all their windows on every floor, every newspaper kiosk seen from the first floor and from the attic, from the front and from an angle. It should be added here that in the rows of windows, on some floor a window will always be found through which instead of a kiosk one can see for instance a large building with a clock tower, since it too belongs to the city, just like fading recollections, unrealized plans, and dreams. Everything that can be thought has its name and – along with the trams, safety pins and rosin – belongs to the city.

Objects and buildings circulate randomly and mingle with one another. Memory must constantly untangle them since permanent order is not possible there. The city can neither be described nor drawn; the reality of the city blocks is resistant to orthogonal projection. Cut off from the sky, deprived of clouds reflected in the window panes, they will rather recall that which remains of streets after they are demolished: an outline of foundations. By manipulating the scale it is possible to create roadways on which the make of a car will squeeze by without difficulty, maybe the color of the bodywork too, but the wheels cannot pass. Every attempt to render a permanent image of the city multiplies similarly defective nooks and crannies which from that instant on assume a life of their own. Thus it is not possible to depict the city in two dimensions regardless of whether they are situated on paper, on a screen or in the memory.

Despite this in any kiosk one can buy a street map of the city, folded into sixteen or thirty-two and marked on the surface by a special configuration that is like a gateway bristling with the black shafts of the letters *W* and *A,* like a great entrance guarding the teeming street names within. These names, printed in the tiniest lettering beneath closed eyes, evoke images of Sunday mornings, autumnal clouds racing across the rooftops, people in overcoats, cracked flagstones in the sidewalk, a music store with cellos in the window, an Alsatian dog with a newspaper in its mouth and a hundred thousand other things. All this breaks off suddenly at the thin line beyond which the white margin begins.

The map also contains train stations, thanks to which it is possible to cross the border of the thin line and conquer the edge of the paper. Trains pass to the outside through dark tunnels concealed beneath the paper. The sides of the wagons carry plywood panels with black inscriptions that cannot be seen in the gloom of the tunnels. The same inscriptions appear on the departure boards. Amongst them are uncommon, beautiful words that make the eyes water slightly. They are written in large letters. The banal ones are written in small letters, for otherwise there would be no room for them – there are a great many of them. Both kinds, however, are but pale reflections of the names toward which the train is headed. It is they that determine the direction of the locomotives on the tangle of tracks invisible under the paper. The true names, those whose force of attraction sets the locomotives in motion, whether beautiful or banal, always lie somewhere beyond the border of the map. It is not known to what degree the cities they refer to really exist.

For nothing in the world is merely invention. Somewhere beyond the margin of the paper lies Żyrardów, which is now a sewing shop, now a spinning mill, now a tannery. Somewhere out there Ożarów, Otwock and Nowy Dwór Mazowiecki, attached to the railroad tracks, by some miracle manage to avoid drifting into space, only because like rosary beads they are threaded with other beads onto strings called the Otwock line, the Skierniewice line, the Nasielsk line. The trains pass through drab neighborhoods where the rumbling of their wheels makes china rattle in the dressers while the tin gutters echo. All the street corners there have been peed on by mongrels and all the mongrels have their tails between their legs. Carts bounce over cobblestones. Patient men stand in line in front of a closed store whose sign has faded in the sun and turned gray from the rain. The streets are filled to the brim with random incidents as if even the mind that gave the city its proper shape broke off at the edge of the map.

Each of these places has its own central point that brings order to its space: It is a lottery office always for the same number game which in essence does not anticipate any winners. It is marked by a sign on which are painted symbols of good luck: a small skinny elephant above a frail four-leaf clover. Yet it is clear the elephant found the cloverleaf too late and is so weakened it cannot eat it. One feels sorry for the elephant because it missed its chance. Apparently somewhere at the furthermost branches of the tracks there live herds of large well-fed elephants that chew on clover – exclusively the four-leaf kind – every day of the week from morning to night till it makes them burp and they get hiccups in the shade of the palm trees. It is warm in both summer and winter where they are, whereas here there is rain and drizzle and dusk falls in the early afternoon. There in that mild climate it is said life is less arduous and death too is easier. An influence of those far-off regions that is hard to explain causes the space around the lottery offices to be distorted and disturbs the arrangement of thoughts as if they were iron filings obedient to the poles of a magnetic field. The contemplation of distant countries leads to serious illness (a trembling of the head and disturbances of vision brought on by a dull pain). Over the magnificent ebb and flow of a storm-whipped sea the color of bottle glass there rise warehouses of corrugated metal, cold landscapes set in window frames. The corrugated metal rises amid weeds; a fly lies upside down in the foreground.

Empty bottles hit passing trains, shatter and remain forever on the embankment, like a testimonial to the mysterious hatred felt by those regions toward anything that moves on tracks: The hatred felt by that which must always stay where it is toward that which – not fastened to the earth – escapes and disappears beyond the horizon.

And yet the tracks, wherever they lead, never forsake the expansive territories of the name even when they pass station buildings bearing innumerable foreign-sounding names such as Radom, Kielce or Kutno painted in black against a white background. Even when they pass through stations with the same names shining in bright colors over gray platforms. The lines of the tracks with their metallic gleam cut straight as arrows across a background black and white like a photograph: Even the wall of red brick has no trace of red in it. They do not attach themselves to any background or to any hue. They glint equally coldly amid fabulously colorful advertising posters, thrown-away illustrated magazines and empty soda cans. It is said that whoever does not know Kutno does not know life. In reality no one knows Kutno and no one ever can know it. The spaces of the name are filled with endless tracks next to which cities form briefly and only when needed and then vanish again immediately afterward like the red lights of semaphores in the gloom of dusk.

The last station turns imperceptibly into a seaport. There without even opening their eyes the passengers can transfer from trains to ships on which they will sail the seven seas. They will see massive whales and fearful icebergs and they will hear the song of sirens. The word *Gdańsk* shining over the platforms can be read as an allusion to a figure wielding a trident against a background of white clouds to the accompaniment of an audible signal. But it may prove only a fragment of a larger whole broken off from the words *Free City Of.* And it may equally well originate from newspaper headlines screaming in the tallest print that no one is willing to die for that name. It is only when its full content is revealed – in the platform sign it has been stintingly replaced with an ambiguous abbreviation – that the gravity of the reference can be comprehended. Yet amongst all the names that can be seen on station platforms there is not one for which the passengers would be prepared to die. The more so because no one knows whether it is possible to die in the same way that one sails the seven seas – without opening one's eyes.

It is for this reason that the places whose names sound from station loudspeakers are incapable of independent existence, even though in many of these names varicolored lights are constantly being turned on and off and there are gigantic perfumed fountains and little silver bells that ring. Is it possible that Paris really exists – a place with a name so pretentious it makes one laugh? Or London, which was essentially conceived as fog? Manchester and Liverpool are two soccer fields with coal tips instead of stands. Bordeaux is a mountain in the shape of a bottle; Rotterdam, Antwerp and the Hague are the names of flea-ridden sailing ships rocking against the quay, their holds filled with spices and silk. Venice is in reality a mother-of-pearl gondola in which is concealed a music box. Chicago is a place filled with suitcases of money where gangsters in felt hats live, shoot guns and die. New York crammed the tallest skyscrapers in the world into an area six inches long and four and a half wide; on the other side there is a box for a postage stamp. Rome is a point to which all roads lead: a dusty moth-eaten inn in the middle of nowhere. The word *Casablanca,* white as paper and black as the night, is the name of a late-night bar for undecided suicides. All these are part of the city and if the truth be told, in it they occupy less room than a bookmark in a book. The passersby who gaze daily at the dim quadrilateral of Constitution Square understand that Paris is where one buys Parisian rolls and that no other Paris exists.

Apparently in Montevideo there is another Constitution Square with palm trees and a fountain in the middle, bathed in the blinding glare of the sun and ringed by colonial mansions. If something like this does exist it is only a supplement to the regular square that everyone knows, an additional hidden aspect of it that escapes everyday attention and does not belong in everyday consciousness. Apparently Milan also has a Central Station in the form of an immense sarcophagus from whose walls stone gargoyles stare down with bulging eyes and bared fangs. This means that for some reason the glass-walled Central Station in the middle of the city needs a more distinct shadow than that cast by its transparent sides. Apparently a Prague of gilded palaces hovers somewhere over the Praga neighborhood of shabby apartment buildings and courtyards deep as wells, cut off from the rest of the city by a river that tastes of rust and engine oil and from the sky of stars by a mantle of clouds and smoke. The buildings, streets and districts are suffocating from opportunities unrealized, transformations uncompleted, promises withdrawn and desires in abeyance for which the city searches in vain for an outlet. In the densely built-up space the city landscapes crowd together; the crush of them oversteps all bounds. It is precisely because of the pressure of missed possibilities that the city begins to generate mirages: the gold of Prague, the mystery of Milan, the colonial architecture of Montevideo.

The Central Station here – the only one that really exists – is one of the principal stops on the routes of the trams as they calmly transport their numbers from one terminus to the other. Hurrying to catch a tram one passes the platforms indifferently since the station is merely an underground passage and a transfer point for the municipal transit system. There are those who are reminded by the sight of the glass walls of when they once bought tickets for a train in the great light-filled hall. But they are well aware that at that time they were dreaming. This magnificent aquarium has no need for platforms or trains; it can exist equally well without them. Nor does it need tram stops or underground walkways. In essence it needs nothing. *It* is the city's salvation.

In the clamorous throng people bend over piles of luggage, lurking like exotic fish on the ooze of the ocean floor; they exchange words that are inaudible amid the hubbub, mutely moving their lips. Others resting their heads against their suitcases gaze at little country stores, at skinny oxen in harness, at a ramshackle truck rattling along a sandy road, yet they do not forget about the bags heaped around them which every so often they must raise their eyelids to count. Their dreams are as unsteady and unsure as the steps of a tightrope walker. At the sound of the loudspeaker they fall, arms flapping, but they do not wake. Staring at green hills and the dry grasses of the steppe, they listen without emotion and without comprehension to announcements about the arrival at various platforms of trains on which they will not leave. Their alien dreams are intertwined with the dreams of this place like warp and weft. Without the partial and hesitant presence of these dreamers the whole would not be complete. In the place of Kazakhstan, Transylvania and at many other points of the city, gaping holes would open up.

This is also the best place in the world for insomniacs, a true sanatorium. For at the station night never falls; evening turns at once into morning, no one knows when. Only here is it possible to look for hope even at the latest hour, to find it and squander it as one sees fit and then hide safely till night outside has passed. There are many insomniacs here. It is time to reveal that it was for them the stations were built. If the insomniacs did not keep vigil night after night the city would fall to pieces for it would be dependent in every way on the dreams of those sleeping. But as is common knowledge night at the station is not really night and dreams are not real dreams and it is only because of this that those hiding in station waiting rooms finally fall asleep, stretched out on the hard benches, at the time when the first trams are already pulling out of the depot.

On the city map the stations look like little rectangles in camouflage colors; there is no sign of the trains that leave – somewhere underneath – for east, west, north and south. Here are the boundless tracks, gleaming iron rails marking the direction through hazy space. The farther it is from the central figure of the map the more vulnerable the order of the world is to disturbance. New branches of railroad routes appear leading toward places that lie neither to the east nor to the west, nor to the north nor to the south. Toward places that are utterly and permanently closed. They cannot be reached by any railroad line despite the fact that they have ticket halls, waiting rooms, platforms and everything that is needed at a station – even arriving and departing trains. One cannot go there by car or even on foot even if one wanted to do so with all one's heart. These are places cut off from the world as if by natural disaster, deprived even of telephone service though there is no lack of telephones there and every post office can receive telegrams. Submerged, there stands in the green waters of memory the city of a month ago, the city of a year ago, the city of forty years ago, each with the last editions of newspapers in its kiosks: meteorological depressions and atmospheric fronts, military parades, influenza epidemics, theater programs and crime reports. This entire space is filled with newsprint. Over every day is suspended a unique configuration of capital letters; unrepeatable shapes are formed by the swarm of lowercase letters, blown away by the winds. Are they not thrown to the winds here every day in their thousands, in their hundreds of thousands?

The city of yesterday and the city of today can seem like a pair of identical-looking pictures from a puzzle in which on closer inspection one may find a flag missing from a rooftop, an additional flowerpot on a windowsill or one more sparrow upon a ledge. There people went to bed in the evening; here they will get up in the morning. Every night, to the rhythm of tomorrow's newspapers revolving on the drums of the rotary presses, the cities of yesterday are rolled up and then vanish. In the morning no trace of them remains. When the new day is over the city will be thoroughly and utterly used up; nothing will be left of it besides the nouns, verbs, adjectives, affirmative and negative sentences drifting everywhere. Yesterday's chair, hat and teapot are already beyond the reach of today's hand, immaterial and unusable. And those who went to bed yesterday evening exist today in the same immaterial way as yesterday's teapots.

The life of today's inhabitants is possible only in one single place in the world: the ephemeral city of today, which differs from the city of yesterday and that of tomorrow in the nature of its substance. Only there can one touch that which lies within reach. Though it may come about that a person will no longer touch the next issue of the newspaper. The newspaper is there but the person is not. This absence indicates that the resemblance between the two pictures in the puzzle means nothing beyond a chance convergence. If however the pictures have already faded then the multitude of visible differences will be so great that recognition will remain in the realm of uncertainty. Here is the square in which the crowd undulates in dance on a summer evening lit by the sun's afterglow or where shivering soldiers trample the snow in the gloom of winter, warming their hands at a brazier. Here is the wind blowing yellow leaves across the empty viewing platform – then how did a Renaissance palace appear in the same place? The possibilities are boundless; it is not hard to imagine cities without a single detail in common. By waiting a sufficiently long time it is even possible to encounter an image of the city with the Eiffel Tower standing amid extensive lawns and flowerbeds with a view of the Arc de Triomphe. It would seem unlikely that the name of such a city would include so many *W*s and *A*s at once. Yet does the Eiffel Tower not suggest a letter *A* itself? And there will always be intermediate cities in which the Arc de Triomphe rises quite unremarkably in the middle of Constitution Square. Every change is simply a matter of time.

And what is time? Those asking have a right to know; they have a right to drum their fingers on the tabletop as they wait for a reply. But the reply does not come. Changes are the only trace that time leaves. What is it made of; how does it flow? Is it like string unwound from a reel or like the knife that cuts the string into pieces? It is that which turns the cogs of clocks or that which the clocks crush in their cogs? Amid the inscriptions chiseled on gateways and the notices pasted on the walls of underpasses, amid advertising catchwords, price lists and election slogans, amid the tangle of sentences unmarked by the slightest shadow of doubt, the one sentence that would resolve the preceding question is missing. The answer was not incorporated into the plans for the city. When its shape was being decided, as attempts were being made to combine the principle of the rectangle with the principle of the star, clocks had only just started to work and no one yet knew anything about time. And when the passage of time revealed the ignorance of the inhabitants the city was already governed by the rule of the meander. Nowhere could one encounter either straight lines or a clear relation between cause and effect, and it became impossible to investigate the truth about the nature of the main construction.

Whatever the mechanism known as time is like, it keeps the machinery in constant motion and through countless gears moves the sun, stars and clouds. Perhaps it operates like steam, depressing pistons, or like compressed gas, the product of the burning of diesel fuel, setting in motion the main V-belt which being a V-belt turns in a circle having neither beginning nor end. It may also be that time is nothing more than change: the shifting of creaking gears; mere revolutions without pistons, steam or flywheel; mere movement without sky or clouds; mere appearance and disappearance. No more than the addition of layers on the trunk of a tree and the growing of new shoots by the branches.

In the dense crown of the tree it is impossible to see where one branch ends and the next begins; there are so many of them intertwined and jumbled together, including those cut off long ago, leaving only knots. For nothing in the world can be cut off completely and finally. The work of the pruning shears brings the proper semblance of order but no improvement can be discerned. The farther away from the trunk one looks the smaller and thinner the branches are; the smaller and thinner they are the more there are of them. The most numerous are next year's branches, so tiny and thin that they are not even visible. The unbridled confusion of the tree prevents one from understanding the purposefulness of the machinery's movement. Yet understanding the movement of the machinery turns the tree into a crude construction of wood and bast, a banal arrangement of water circulation.

Everyone knows that *tree* and *machine* are only words; whoever utters them stops the motion of the world for a moment in their head. Thus, along with irritation at this willfulness, in places there arises a temptation to set in order the movement of the world in the heads of those who oversimplify it or render it excessively complicated. But the removed imaginations leave behind scars and hatred. Even if one were to imprison all those who think the world is like a tree, or their adversaries who maintain that it is like a machine; even if they were all to be shot and buried in mass graves, the prisoners, and especially the dead, would be confirmed in their convictions and would become more stubborn and less willing to compromise than ever before. For nothing in the world – even imaginations – can be destroyed completely and finally.

Since nothing can be annulled or removed, in the spaces of the name there still exists the city of excavations peopled by men in rubber boots and women wearing headscarves, the place where this story had its beginning. No change has occurred there, no new house has been finished nor have any more burned-out ruins been pulled down. The vast bomb crater in whose roar everything began has not been filled in. It remains as a trace of the sudden flare that at a certain moment bathed the tenants of the apartment buildings, the owners of glass-fronted cabinets containing china, of escritoires and ottomans. They were bathed in it and then they burned along with their furniture or else they were swallowed up by the earth, lying outstretched, their arms crossed over their chest. So the crater is still there, deep as the caldera of a volcano, and in it a stinking bloody gurgling persists – a welter of dirty bandages, baby carriages, single shoes, crushed hats, rusty scrap metal, trampled eyeglasses. While above it, like volcanic ash, hover feathers from ripped-open pillows.

The people in the rubber boots looked alike, as if they were cast from the same mold. They had arms and legs; they had noses, ears and eyes. It seemed that when they stood in their ranks they must have seen the same things. Yet they barely looked at those things. They each looked in their own direction at memories they preferred to keep to themselves, at scenes that always took place in the foreground against a chance backdrop of scaffolding. They were the children of characters sitting in curved chairs in a photographer's studio or standing in front of sepia-colored trees in all kinds of outfits and headgear: round cloth caps with oilskin peaks, pomponned kepis and pillbox hats and even bowlers and panamas. Along with a physical description the heirs to these images also inherited – like a promissory notice to be paid off – the impermanence of form. Transformed from children into adults and themselves at the mercy of others' recollections, in their own memories they preserved nonexistent addresses and interiors and carried palaces, squares and streets with which they were unable to part. At hand they kept only what was most necessary: watch, suitcase, pocketknife, Primus stove, scarf, pictures of ladies in hats and veils.

One of the most important differences between the city of excavations and the city of memories was that the majority of characters from the photographs were gone. Their eyes – grayish or brownish, staring rather naively from behind their veils at some spring afternoon or perhaps a summer morning that no one remembers anymore – could see neither the excavations nor the people in rubber boots who carried their singed pictures with them. It was not known what had happened to the love that lent a warm tinge to their sepia-colored gaze: whether it had crumbled to dust amid the flames like a china teacup or whether it had blown away with the smoke into the sky.

Gazes, interiors and objects were gradually erased from memories to the extent that observers grew accustomed to new images. Certain things, soot-blackened but undamaged, were taken directly from the ruins. The observers of the changes were convinced that they knew where they came from. In their view they were from the city of furnishings where they had once been seen. They assumed that the things had somehow found their way out of the aforementioned crater, perhaps expelled by it along with the rubble and the ashlike lava. Yet if this is true, in such a manner barely one typewriter in a thousand, only one china teacup out of fifty thousand, made it from the city of furnishings to the city of excavations. Where were the other thousands of typewriters and china teacups? The fact was that they were no longer anywhere: neither on the earth nor below the earth nor in the air.

At this point the obvious truth should be mentioned: The inhabitants of the city of excavations were also not from here. They too crawled out from the crater, filthy, smoke-blackened, in rags. There was no return to the place they had come from. They were born in the immediate or distant vicinity of the mass of tapering Ws and As, in regions through which there passes a dark and turbid stream bearing the image of those same letters, recognizable yet indistinct, like steep roofs or pencil-thin steeples. In the city of excavations different Ws and As gazed at their reflection in the river; they were somewhat similar to the others, but more like steeples with their tops snapped off, burned-out roofs, lone apartment buildings surrounded by piles of rubble.

But since nothing in the world can be completely and finally destroyed it is clear that the letters written on the water still exist somewhere and will continue to do so forever along with the city abounding in fragile teacups and flammable furniture, the city of the grotesque, safe, entirely free of disasters and unsusceptible to pathos. Whoever recalls its misfortunes has to laugh: Its sorrow has a false bottom in which merriment is concealed. A lot of space there is occupied by New York, with paper shares swirling in the air like petals, populated by financiers jumping out of the windows of skyscrapers, and New Orleans where black men in white tuxedos play golden saxophones at all hours of the day and night, and London where there are crowds of bankers in bowler hats, urbane criminals, detectives in checkered cycling caps and police inspectors from Scotland Yard moving their lips silently to the rhythm of ragtime music played on out-of-tune upright pianos thrust into the corner under the screen. For in this city there is a movie theater on every street and a piano in every theater. That is why it is swarming with portly industrialists with a monocle in one eye hunting for a wife and trying to marry off their daughters. Bands play tangos for them; tuxedoed waiters bustle around them and the doormen bow low. Here there is everything needed in life: horse races, air shows, military parades and roulette. While in the background fashionable men with small mustaches take the air, a schoolgirl in eyeglasses wanders by and a child newspaper vendor with a cigarette in his mouth hawks his wares.

Within the frame there is no room for what the industrialists never need: rundown stores with no sign or window display, selling matches, shoelaces and cheap soap: things none of those fat genial fellows would ever dream of buying. The anemic storekeepers are doomed to inevitable bankruptcy; there is no hope for the tailors with their many children, masters of the art of turning well-worn garments, nor for the cobblers who can take a pair of boots worn to shreds and turn them into one brand-new shoe. Spurned by the elegant public, they are starving. Their brilliant work is known only to those who cannot afford it. The capricious eye seeks out gleaming signboards and large glass windowpanes behind which are flaunted all possible models, patterns and styles that can be thought up in this city of endless entertainment. Here no frill bears the weight of final things and final things are not anticipated at all. Even those who jump off the bridge into the river do so for banal and laughable reasons.

Can it be said then of this feather-light city that of its buildings not one stone was left upon a stone? Rather they crumbled to the four winds. The latest models, patterns and styles which the world had doted on simply evaporated. They were destroyed at least to the extent that even in recollection they proved strikingly unfashionable. Yet they were destroyed – like everything in the world – only partially. For what is fashion? That which makes a hat with a broad brim and adorned with artificial fruit one day start to look ridiculous, so it becomes clear that it must be replaced with a tiny toque. For a moment everyone believes sincerely that toques will always remain what they are: appropriate in every regard.

The stage of the memory is equipped with panoramas rolled up beneath the ceiling, on which there is a permanent record of the transitory configurations of shop signs, monuments and municipal gardens. In the memory's submerged theater the empty rows of seats are overgrown with algae. In the standing water everything has its place. The city of toques in window displays becomes completely covered over when all of a sudden from the ceiling there falls the canvas of the next panorama, unrolling as it falls and painted with piles of bricks. The toques arouse pity and it becomes obvious that they must be replaced with headscarves tied beneath the chin.

Behind, yet another panorama is hidden, the one for which large hats with artificial fruit are appropriate: the city of shop signs in two languages, a city glistening with muddy puddles and smelling of must, animals and blood. Against its background there rises a perpetual fog, while a procession moves forward bearing crosses and banners; Cossack horsemen in fur hats raise their swords, the hand of a thief removes a wallet from someone's pocket and there can be heard the whistle of bullets frozen in midair and the whinnying of horses rearing on their hind legs. After the rain little boys, the illegitimate sons of cooks and firemen, sail paper boats on the frothing streams in the gutters. In this city two train stations stand on either side of the river, each sending forth its own separate railroad network. Between these two rail networks a connecting line is unthinkable. The only possible connection turns out to be a horse-drawn tram that shuttles between the two stations across the entire city, crossing the bridge that spans the river.

This city is built of a twofold kind of imagination to which the two rail networks correspond. One extends toward Moscow and St. Petersburg, the other toward Paris and Lausanne. They are unable to pass beyond the city gates, which does not prevent them from entwining the whole world with their networks – spreading farther every year – and acquiring locomotive sheds, warehouses and provincial garrisons in which it is possible to embezzle the regimental funds and then shoot one-self in the head.

In this city there live sand-diggers who seek consolation at the pub on the corner, and clerks in threadbare frock coats who quail beneath the gaze of their superiors and who have no future in their offices since all the best positions are permanently occupied by jovial old men or cynical young swells; bearded Jews, blacksmiths and carpenters from failing shops, self-aggrandizing engineers, and coughing poets devoid of inspiration. They are passed on the street by carriages containing disdainful generals in white uniforms embroidered with gold thread, and by the steeds of cheerful lieutenants separated by hundreds of versts from their mothers and sisters, uncertain whether the mud beneath their horses' hooves can be real in a place that is so accidental and in which the only self-evident thing is the garrison.

The area enclosed by the gates is rather cramped. To cross from one end to the other takes half an hour, forty-five minutes in bad weather; the trip leaves no illusions. Certain inhabitants of the city, sick of its narrow horizons, attempted to perish in flames or in snows. Others, equally distressed, decided that it was their duty to live there and that death was a kind of layoff. Both the former and the latter, from the cradle to the grave, when they reached for something with their hand would encounter empty space and when they took a step would bump into a wall. The first perished the way they wanted – in snows or in flames. The second died in unaired rooms, their bedside tables littered with tiny bottles containing bitter medicines, leeches behind their ears. But death could not soothe their pain.

Both the former and the latter ultimately came to rest in caskets; the caskets crumbled to dust deep beneath the earth yet the pain remained on the surface: in stuffy bedrooms, in pubs on the corner, in sofas on which they used to sit, in drawers where their letters were kept. Eventually the day came when the sofas were chopped up for firewood; a stray shell released the letters from their drawers. Paper turned to ashes, window-panes shattered, door frames and tiled stoves were smashed to pieces. But this too failed to stop the pain. For pain does not belong to those who experience it but rather they belong to it. Taking into its possession successive tradesmen, clerks and poets, it fills all interiors to the very ceiling.

Many tried to flee from it, surreptitiously taking advantage of the fact that every unaired room contains broad plains over which great clouds sail past, and endless tracts across which coaches drawn by galloping horses deliver documents that bear a two-headed eagle on their seals. Certain inhabitants of this city desired space so badly that they abandoned the city forever. They were sucked in by the wide-open spaces of boundless fields, which in order to exist needed the tracks of the railroad that spread from year to year, from station to station, to the very end, where it transpired there was no way back. They began to wander aimlessly about St. Petersburg, great in its golden frame, where beneath the shiny varnish it is dark in the winter for as much as twenty hours a day. Or Moscow, where the streets were paved with wood that may have been real or may have been made from lacquered building blocks. They even traveled as far as Tula, which was tall and had a brass tap to let out boiling water, and also to Omsk and Tomsk, where in the summertime they float wood down the river and in winter they are chilled to the marrow. And to Astrakhan – that storehouse of ice and skins – where caviar is eaten by the spoonful and champagne drunk straight from the bottle. At the feet of a good few of these lost travelers, somewhere at the meeting point of steppe and sea there opened up a dark abyss by the name of Odessa, filled with sailors, bandits, officers and femmes fatales, washed over beyond salvation by waves of epidemics and filled forever with the echo of shots. Some did not stop till Baku, where blood flows like rainwater in the streets, or Khabarovsk, where White Army soldiers without boots lie on the white snow. Or Vladivostok, that last station in the world, toward which tracks that previously ran straight as an arrow begin to describe the first loop of a spiral. The next loop rests on Harbin, where Chinese in felt shoes wade through snowdrifts. Subsequent loops are no longer visible; one has only to hold on ever more tightly on the curves. Saved or lost, people sucked into the vortex were swept into the interior of memories and began to live as the recollections of others, endlessly repeating their former gestures. Younger than they were in their youth, they looked from their nightstands through eyes that saw nothing at all: neither the space nor the flames.

The city the inhabitants know is composed of a certain number of elements that have a defined color and shape but do not possess a permanent location. They move about, vanishing then emerging again, like crystals in a kaleidoscope. Here, for nannies minding children there opens up a park surrounded by a cast-iron fence, here a great hotel presents itself, having previously demolished the stables of the light-horse barracks. Somewhere there rises an Orthodox church with a dome like a crystal that till now has been hidden behind others. One day Russian lettering disappears from the shop signs and is replaced with Gothic script. The streets bear now one set of names, now another. The statues on the plinths change; the fountain in the square is pulled down because an underground passageway is being built, and reappears many years later in a different place. The crystals move about in disorder, and it is only the arrangement of the mirrors that creates the illusion of regular, perfectly symmetrical wholes in which the element of the accidental temporarily acquires the status of principal structural component. The city is a work of the eyes. In them as in mirrors the random configurations of colored crystals are reflected and thus acquire symmetry and sense. A scratch on the glass, an unforeseen glint, a speck of dust, subjected to the same rule, multiplied and incorporated into the whole, defines the context. It is precisely in this way that Moscow and St. Petersburg appear here and also Paris and Lausanne: as optical illusions produced by blemishes in mirrors. It goes without saying that even the slightest movement of the elements must lead to significant changes in Paris and St. Petersburg. The shadow of a mote of dust on the mirror is sufficient for the cancan to begin in the cabarets; it may also alter the cut of full-length overcoats. Not to mention a good shake, which makes the crystals pile up and then scatter. The sudden appearance of an inconceivable connecting line between the two railway stations will threaten the equilibrium of the whole. The city, pulled in two directions, will incline dangerously toward Paris, where the Trans-Siberian Railroad is a paper share, one of many noted on the stock exchange, and where every day at dusk the terraces of the cafés are filled with laughing people who have never heard of it.

Many a Paris is inhabited by sentimental residents of St. Petersburg dressed in hotel livery, dexterously pocketing tips and surreptitiously wiping away tears of emotion, while one of the successive St. Petersburgs may turn out to be a provincial backwater completely invisible from beneath another name as beneath thick wrapping paper, a place that the inhabitants of Paris never visit. And yet even the tiniest scrap of wrapping paper amid the crystals of the kaleidoscope would suffice for the whole to take on a grayish coloration and a gloomy atmosphere, for wrapping paper utterly changes the properties of light.

It is possible to imagine a city perfect in its entirety, a city that is the sum of all possibilities. In it nothing is missing and nothing can perish; every china teacup comes from somewhere and is destined for somewhere. But precisely this absolute city is eaten away by the sickness of never-ending disasters. Change invariably brings confusion to the lives of the inhabitants. One has to pay attention so as not to drive accidentally onto a bridge that was demolished years ago, so as not to sit on the terraces of torn-down cafés once known for their unparalleled doughnuts. Long hours can be wasted waiting at the stops of long-canceled tram routes if one does not notice at once that the rails have been covered over with asphalt. One has to remember carefully where walls have been put up that once were not there. Crossing a market square filled with carts and horses with bags of oats round their necks, it is best not to forget about the nature of apartment buildings and about the opaqueness and firmness of their interior walls. That which one can bump into and hurt oneself on from a certain perspective is more real than the fleeting landscapes seen by a gaze turned in on the interior of the memory. The present moment slips through the fingers of the inhabitants of the city of changes; they must thus live by means of the past. They merely try not to knock their heads against the walls out of nostalgia for that which is no longer. They realize that it is not the walls that block their view. Even if they destroyed them with their gaze the marketplace with its horses and carts still would not return to its place. They would have too much to lose, considering that the alleyways, transparent as air, made by the cuboids that form an invisible frontage would be filled with a vacuum that with a whistle would suck in crumpled newspapers, umbrellas, hats, and recollections.

Lesser wholes can be more easily encompassed with the gaze. Every one of the supplementary cities hovers freely in space, as weightless and incorporeal as an image in a kaleidoscope. They are not linked by pipes or cables through which substance or energy could flow. They neither appear nor disappear, nor change into one another. Each exists for itself and is closed in on itself – and nothing in them ever changes. It is precisely because they endure so immutably that there has to be so many of them. But observers, who cannot get by without ordering events in their memory, try to combine them into a single whole so as to restore to the world its continuity and its consequentiality, its cause and effect. It is because of them that what is new becomes old and what is clean becomes dirty. The city seen by the observers is a place in which today's dust falls on yesterday's dust, in which bread goes stale, water dries up and iron rusts. There statues are erected and knocked down, while streets bear now one name, now a different one. The city woven from changes is a stage for perpetual entrances and exits that deteriorates a little more with every day, a place of losing and finding, breaking and mending, birth and death.

Past events leave traces in the memory like an ax chopping wood. Chips fly; they remain where they fall even after the wood has been used to light the stove. Trampled underfoot and rained upon, they slowly change color. If nothing can be preserved and saved, how are recollections supposed to resist changes? In this city of changes, ruled by memory, there had to be room for everything that memory has retained, yet every day its contents are reduced to shreds a little more. As if in a wardrobe where alongside an off-the-rack suit of low-grade wool there hangs a moldering yet good-quality uniform of a now defunct regiment, and between them a lady's muff infested with moths.

It is for this reason that the spaces yawning inside heads are vaster than anything that can be thought up. Every one of the past and future cities thrust into the recesses of the world has its own star there, and it can also be said that each of these cities is the most important one. For is the world not composed exclusively of recesses? As is common knowledge some stars have been extinguished; a certain number of them were destroyed by stray helicopters. But the name guards the city against collapse, since it has the property of containing within itself all that was and is no longer and all that has been told to the marines.

Prey to longing and doubt, every night the unquiet city of recollections releases dreams – enchanted adhesive shoots that seek support in silence and darkness. Yet they find nothing but other dreams, and so the dreams attach to one another. They grow in all directions, creating knots and loops, twining around one another, merging together and then branching. There are dark dreams and bright dreams, beautiful dreams and horrible dreams. But their brightness always arises from darkness and their beauty from horror. The tangle of dreams, untouched by pruning shears, fills the whole world; it can even be said that *it* is the world and that the inhabitants of the city – along with their houses, their beds, their blankets, their recollections and their unanswerable questions – are only necessary for the dreams to be dreamed.

Only for dreams to be dreamed? What about maintaining order in the world? What about polishing floors, making repairs? Surely the reason why people sleep at night is to gather strength for the labors of the day? Well, in fact this is not so. It is not enough to sleep soundly and eat well. It would always transpire that bread from dreams is not filling, that water from dreams does not quench one's thirst. Dreams – those merry or cheerless realms of unfulfillment – were able to open the inhabitants' eyes to the whole truth which always escaped them in their waking hours: that the desire to maintain order in the world also arises from dreams. From strenuous dreams in which every object the eye lights upon finds its place, while five others are scattered and lost at the same time. But the dreamers cannot see this since they dream inattentively.

At dusk the city of dreams and the city extending in space become one and join in a murky whole crowned by the black silhouettes of office buildings against a reddish sky, giantedifices constructed not long ago yet already affected by corrosion and darkness. Nowhere is there any boundary marker, inscription or informational sign that would indicate the relative positions of dreams and waking life. Some take the ringing of alarm clocks in the morning as a signal indicating the crossing of the border. But alarm clocks which themselves belong to dreams cannot wake people from them.

In the depths of sleep the dreamers push their way into trams, from trams into offices, from offices into stores. Dreaming, they wander amongst the shelves and squint at the overabundance of colors and shapes. The plenitude muddles their heads. In every item there dwells a promise; the future changes as the dreamers carry their shopping along. The immaculate beauty of an altered fate endures for a short moment after the parcels are unpacked, then melts away without a trace. But the everyday lack of hope lying in wait for the happy purchasers in the corners of apartments is not allowed in the city of dreams. Each inhabitant can have the sins of their life – their uncertainty and sorrow – accounted for by the unknown women and men who have a guaranteed livelihood on the vast surfaces of billboards. They live amongst appropriate slogans, calm and immobile. They are given assurances about which no one else is able even to dream.

In the city of dreams all the colors of cars are reflected in the glossy floors of automobile salesrooms. Passersby are thrilled as they look through the huge display windows: they admire the nobility and the power. The sales managers watch over the cars. Passersby who wish to sit behind the wheel and drive off must have with them a bag full of cash or a certified bank check. And so many inhabitants of the city of dreams, unable to count on their check being certified, instead wander day and night in search of bags filled with money.

It is they who crowd into buildings equipped with special openings in the roof and internal chutes to direct the rain of money directly to devices that count it and divide it, according to their needs, amongst those waiting for a miraculous decree of fate. Every number, color and card must win sooner or later. The wheel of fortune spins only so that everyone should receive a generous share. Those who do not come empty-handed will not regret it if they wait long enough for their lucky moment and at just the right instant do not hesitate to put everything on a single card. It is precisely here – and nowhere else – that one can catch hold of destiny, by one's own hand correct its crooked rudder without wasting time and energy on other actions that are indirect and of dubious effectiveness. But the game must be paid for. One single coin is needed, the lucky one. Whoever has already used up their coin will not win. It is better then not to raise one's eyes so as not to be tempted to buy chewing gum, peanuts and beer. But those who play are certain of nothing, not even that. Everyone wasted their lucky coin long ago on trifles. That is why the rain of money from the sky that falls into the special openings in the roof is ultimately drained off into the sewers.

The city of dreams never forgets about money. In the evening its glow spreads across the sky over immense hotels. Elevators glistening with chrome and nickel bear smug foreigners in gleaming shoes and silk underwear, with fat wallets tucked in the inside pockets of their soft woolen suits. A mist of cologne mingles with cigar smoke and the aroma of freshly brewed coffee. As high as the clouds, the skyscrapers stand in a row with walls made of huge sheets of glass, behind which lobbies filled with leather sofas and tropical greenery are lit in the glow of thousands of lamps. Whoever crosses the threshold of these hotels immediately becomes a foreigner and can leave forever for America, above the clouds, a lit cigar in his mouth. Yet if he reaches into the inside pocket of his jacket he will be disappointed – nothing is there.

For the most impatient, there are numerous recruiting offices for the Foreign Legion; in each of them, day and night, a French-speaking officer blows smoke rings as he puffs on his pipe. He wears a white kepi and a uniform with red and green facings in which he fought in the desert and stumbled through sandstorms. Whoever enters there, even by mistake, he presents with a contract to sign, binding him to fifteen years' service in the tropics, and shows him on his fingers in round sums the amount his government will pay the volunteer. He entices with the green of hope and with an indifferent smile conceals his embarrassment at the presence, next to the green facings, of blood red. Blood that the passerby signing the contract will shed in the tropics. The foreign officer is well aware that in the tropics it is possible to live entirely without blood; in case of need it can be replaced with cognac, which is supplied by the caseload to the mess halls there. The round sums paid to the volunteer by the foreign government will be put toward its purchase, since in the tropics it is not possible to live without cognac. And having signed the contract the passerby disappears for good, because from the tropics no one ever returns.

The disillusioned, who have already tried everything, have too little time to dream of America or the tropics and too little strength to search far and wide. They walk into the first bank they come across and cast a tired glance at the teller; in a split second he understands their demand, backed up by the glint of oxidized steel. A bag is filled with banknotes and no unnecessary words are spoken; no one will trouble their head about a receipt. And so some dreams resound with the wail of police sirens and the squeal of tires. They are filled with hair-raising chases and interminable breakneck escapes. The dreamers hold on to the steering wheel for dear life and stare fixedly ahead, while bridges, trees and banknotes whistle past in the wind. They come to a stop in a blind alley where escapes and chases turn out to be a matter of life and death. A hand reaches for a gun, an eye looks down the barrel and a shot rings out: hit or miss. No one can predict which it will be.

Choking from the tension, the city of dreams could not exist without its cellars, the heart of which is the percussion. Its rhythm thrills the hearts of the audience, tormented by sorrow, longing and fury. In the deafening noise fury erupts in red, longing in green and sorrow in blue. Anyone who buys a ticket has a right to expect enlightenment. But the moment people enter they are plunged in shadow. There are as many of those seeking enlightenment as could fit in, and each has brought their own darkness. It spills out through the pupils of their eyes and floods the entire place, including the bottles behind the bar, the gaudy makeup and the hundreds of outfits belonging to desperately grasping gazes. The lights flash on and off, summoning from the gloom isolated grimaces and gestures and for a moment revealing their strangeness to the world. In reality there is not even any percussion here. It had to be replaced with a record spinning on the mechanical turntable of a gramophone; everyone knows this and no one cares. The true heart of this place is the sound of the percussion alone. It does not subdue the pulsing of blood in the temples and does not alleviate true fury, longing or sorrow, but it smoothes grimaces and softens gestures. Burdens vanish; those dancing acquire a lightness that outside of this place they could not even dream of. The love that takes refuge in the sound of the percussion is so devoid of weight that it can only be a shadow of love, something that takes up no room whatsoever in the heart; something as imper-manent as sound and, like sound, incapable of being taken out-side or kept for later. For this reason couples leaving for any of the neighboring rooms – the barroom, the delivery room or the courtroom – have to get by without love.

Yet without love those dreaming lack the strength to dream on, and even more to wake up. They manage as best they can. They buy neckties on elastic bands that are easier to take off when one's collar digs into one's neck and one's head is splitting with pain. They buy headache tablets that bring them relief but harm their stomach. So they buy pills for stomachache that cause pains in their liver. Everything goes for nought. They renounce their heart, stomach and liver as superfluous ballast that drags them to the ground; they pawn them for credit and, shuffling their feet, they return to where they were looking at automobiles. It is not clear how the fleets of cars leave the show-rooms. The doorways are too narrow and the display windows too high. There is no avoiding scratches on the gleaming paint-work. The luster of newness disappears at once. The farther they drive the worse they look. They can be seen later, mud-spattered and rusty, driving from one suburb to another and back, the clutch snapped off, without wheels or engine, smash-ing into one another. The inhabitants of the city of dreams curse the cars and curse the misleading promises on the bill-boards. In other posters they seek new more reliable promises and dream with their remaining strength, choosing the worst solutions like a drowning man, who as everyone knows will grasp at a straw.

In the hospitals of the city of dreams there are trays filled with surgical instruments with the aid of which rib cages are opened and closed as easily as boxes. But people who live for years without heart or liver eventually become embittered misanthropes whose organisms develop increasing numbers of special requirements because of which an operation has no chance of success. At visiting times individuals with shifty eyes loiter in the hallways; they hide from the white-aproned medical personnel and, whispering to the patients' families, offer to buy what is needed, under the counter, without involving scalpels or operating theaters. The patients receive cash for hearts in which a little love is still left or livers that are not entirely used up, convinced that they just got the best deal of their lives. Then they open brokerage agencies and wholesale warehouses. Some of them die happily in the warehouse accounting room; others collapse suddenly in their own office, telephone receiver in hand. They too cannot be helped by the operating theaters of the city of dreams. The forceps, generally so useful in closing vessels cut open by the scalpel, do not possess the necessary teeth for seizing and holding life as it fades away.

There is no solution in the world so bad that no one will chose it. Even the worst way out may prove the best for someone. There exist higher purposes: for example, never under any circumstances to leave the city of dreams. And for this its inhabitants are prepared to pay any price since between one dream and the next an abyss opens up beneath them that they are more afraid of than anything else in the world: the black chasm of sleep without dreams. Not for an instant do they tear their gaze away from the flickering lights that otherwise would have to be extinguished in the twinkling of an eye. Colors, shapes and sounds change from one moment to the next, but the city of dreams does not force anyone to choose between them. Its inhabitants believe that given propitious circumstances, they can have everything at once: love, American cigars, the gold of the banks and the heat of the tropics. They do not however want the stillness of waking hours, the tedium of which destroys any pleasure that may arise from being one thing or another, from trying on outfits, choosing one's words, employing irony or pathos. Yet are dreaming and being awake not merely two different ways of living in this city? Two ways of living that alternate twice a day? This is what some believe. They imagine that sleeping and waking are like obverse and reverse of a coin or, better, like the two hemispheres of the moon, the light and the dark. They forget that the moon always shows them the same hemisphere: the brightly lit hemisphere of dreams.

THIS CITY WAS BUILT AT THE MEETING POINT OF THREE elements in a place where they mingled with one another. It was constructed on the clay of memories, on the sands of dreams and on the ground waters of oblivion, cold and black, whose flow never ceases for a moment, washing away the foundations day after day. In their swirling depths the coins of distinctions vanish. The sunken coins apparently have power over oblivion; lying on the bottom, they preserve the memory of events and places. But it is not known how they can protect, since they themselves perish in the miry ooze beneath which obverse and reverse look the same. There the stillness of waking hours does not prevent the agitation of dreams, or vice versa. The waters of oblivion are not ruled by any rational principle and for this reason they reconcile all inconsistencies.

Differentiations! Life and death, tree and machine, beginning and end! Every name like a coin has its obverse and reverse. When paying with a coin it is not possible to spend half of it, keeping either the heads or the tails for oneself. All that is large is small and vice versa. Ambiguity is a consequence of calling things by their names. Every name teeters on a knife edge, in desperation, and makes differentiations necessary. Every adjective that is juxtaposed with it will bring along a counteradjective, every conjecture a counterconjecture. good will create evil, warmth will create cold, end will create beginning. Whoever maintains that the world resembles a tree is the enemy and brother of him who insists that it resembles a machine. Both know what a tree is and what a machine is. In attempting to touch the essence of things they keep using the same names as if they were arguing about some precious plunder, torn apart by the desire to keep the whole lot but in agreement about the amount and the name of the currency; at the same time they will hear nothing about counterfeit banknotes. But whoever describes the city in a hundred thousand words will nourish a hundred thousand words of the countercity and each of them will return to the city like a bad penny.

No one asks where nouns come from or who they belong to. The inhabitants of the city carry them with complete confidence, just as in its beginning they carried bricks, convinced that they were laboring for themselves and their children and that whoever bears the burden is its owner. At one time they cheered as records were beaten on scaffolding and believed that the hand lifts the brick, not the opposite. They have always yielded easily to illusions. In their own opinion they are the masters of words, yet words do not obey them. They do not stick to objects; they suddenly change meaning or disappear, replaced by other words. They move, now here now there, dragging thoughts, questions and desires behind them.

Though people here burden themselves with anything the eye can see, they have no possessions. The objects they have bought or received as presents always eventually vanish or are destroyed. Their clothes, though they were new, end up being old, their children turn into adults. In recollections there remain only nouns, verbs and adjectives, like deposit slips, but the things listed on them have long since gone from any warehouse.

The inhabitants of the city clutch their slips and believe themselves the owners of countless possessions; they have no intention of giving up a single thing, even the snows of yesteryear. Like travelers who, depositing their suitcases at the left-luggage office, walk about the city, they are certain that their belongings are at their disposal at every moment. Where is that vast left-luggage office containing plush teddy bears that belonged to soldiers, the happy moments of abandoned women, the fortunes of bankrupts, the kisses of those run over by trams, the reflections of sunsets in windowpanes, finished melodies and eaten tarts? Here it is: It is great and small; without any difficulty it contains all this, though it itself fits easily on a shelf, in a hard cover, with an alphabetical list of entries. In it tart is next to tartan, and like it has the black color of printer's ink.

The naming of things never brought anyone happiness. Yet despite this, names circulate without ceasing, ever more densely and feverishly. For what has not been named drifts away on the waves of the river. Everything takes flight. Events do not attach to words and do not need them in order to flow. They roll through the city, stirring up shoals of glittering definitions, describing every moment in various ways. What is supposed to flow, flows, while definitions remain in place, rocking on the waves, tied down with ropes, round and brightly colored, like buoys on the river. The inhabitants of the city use them to mark the course of events in order to understand them better. This is a necessity: Events by their nature are incomprehensible, with a tendency to overflow in all directions and efface their borders. Love requires white veils, black tuxedos and beribboned limousines, but at times it must make do with a grille in the visiting room. Sleep requires a room and a bed but in extremity it can manage with a bench in a station waiting room or even a corner of the sidewalk, thus becoming something that can be confused with fainting, drunkenness or death. It is precisely because of this that navigational signs – the buoys of words – are so essential. It is they that make it possible to differentiate, to separate out that which would be jumbled up. One beside the other, they bob up and down on the waves of events, obscuring them entirely. It is not surprising that in the end their movement is taken for the waves themselves, and that descriptions conceal objects.

Even events themselves are not needed to set flowing that which is meant to flow. In fact only words are essential. Thus on a rainy day an incautious pedestrian dies at a busy intersection and a drunk driver causes a fatal accident, from one moment to another becoming a criminal. The family, plunged into sorrow, bids farewell forever to a father and grandfather, a teacher of many years, while children carry their ink-stained backpacks to school and rejoice at the fact that their test has been canceled. The police escort the culprit from the lockup to the courtroom; at the same time a taxicab is taking a woman in labor in the opposite direction to the maternity clinic. If someone should desire a telephone connection between the courthouse and the delivery room it is technically feasible, but the gaudy, hollow buoys of words that mark roles and the course of matters render such a telephone a needless waste of time, a caprice and even a suspicious subterfuge, a trick employed in bad faith. The words *criminal* and *escort* fix figures in their roles, in freeze frame. Names delimit the boundaries of what is possible. On a different day, another person dies at the same intersection; in the courtroom, another trial begins (the escort and the arrestee have the same journey to make, though the section numbers from the criminal code cited in the charge sheet are different). A woman in labor rides to the maternity clinic in a taxicab; perhaps rain is falling again; the same children carry their backpacks to school and, on the way, are gradually imbued with the mournfulness of grammar and of exercises involving trains. The victims of accidents, the police officers, criminals, schoolchildren, the women in labor and the cab drivers have no choice: They have to make their way in the direction laid out by the street, to enter and exit through doors, and to do so during the hours they are open. They never come into the world or die, except in connection with the circumstances that precede these events and then follow them; they are utterly bound by rules determined by the relations between words. Nothing will occur that cannot be named, and everything that can be named will sooner or later occur.

Events do not stop even for a minute in their course. They carve out bends and uncover islands. The flowing water sculpts the banks – the only memento it leaves behind. Where the greatest number of accidents occurred an underground passageway has been constructed. Where things were bought and sold marketplaces have sprung up; where thieves gathered a police station has been built. Even soccer matches and loud concerts leave behind colored marks on the walls. Everywhere there is a multitude of signs aiding memory, and telling gaps where the signs have been removed or destroyed.

Calling things by their names helps only briefly. Everything named also falls into oblivion, because tomorrow each word will be needed again for something else. Events for which words escape everyone will fall into oblivion first. Faded definitions are like lost deposit slips – the recollections to which they refer can no longer be retrieved. Oblivion wipes away gestures and grimaces; it wipes away chased clouds, raindrops on windows, gusts of wind. Inhabitants of the city try to create new words that will be more convenient than the old ones – but they try in vain. The new words are no improvement, and just like the old ones they obey no one's will. The city of changes was created by memory in search of needles in haystacks. It is utterly dependent on recollections, those castles in the sand washed away by tidewaters. Harried by the waves of oblivion, it requires inhabitants that bear within themselves thoughts, questions and desires in which city landscapes are embedded – so that the city might remember itself.

The eyes of passersby gaze every day upon underground passageways, marketplaces and police stations. They gaze upon inscriptions on walls and in stairwells. The hand resting on the banister feels beneath its fingers the old chipped enamel. It is in this way that everyday thoughts are recovered. These are for the most part small and hard morning thoughts that contain the tiniest possible questions or no questions whatsoever. They hide in clothing, in objects, in furniture, differently from evening thoughts, whose sharp little needles are stuck beneath skulls for memory's sake. The walls of stairwells are marked by streaks and stains, each one from something different, some already very old. Certain thoughts for which there was no room elsewhere can be so completely absorbed into the shape of a stain that one encounters them every time one climbs or descends the stairs. Thanks to this they endure, saved for some time yet from oblivion. Later it transpires that the same stain has come to mean something else. The language of stains is impoverished and slipshod. The same shapes have to convey contradictory meanings. But these meanings themselves are so slipshod and impoverished that the shapes of the stains seem only too good for them.

Though this is not a rule, more significant thoughts may take on the shape of a large object, for instance a tram standing at a stop. At such times they drive off with the tram, leaving memory with the impossible task of searching for them. And it is only this task that keeps together the round billion of dark red bricks. The city of changes, constructed by memory and destroyed by oblivion, is a city of death.

The tide of death spares only the stone bricklayers and foundrymen in their stone clothing, gazing at the traffic with stone eyes from their alcoves. For the kind of life they have within themselves is not subject to destruction even in floods, fires or the demolition of buildings. A broken-off stone head can continue to exist; it is no more motionless than when it was attached to a neck. An isolated hand remains as inactive as when fastened to a forearm. An index finger remains the same even at the bottom of the river, half-buried in mud and entwined with algae. Even crushed stone spread on roads has its weight and volume and its position in space.

The life of stones is entirely free of coercion. When they lose support they fall down. Having fallen they lie there. True, they have no influence over the form they are given; but they accept it with absolute indifference. With the same indifference they endure or crumble. Whatever happens they will never add anything from themselves. They never contribute the slightest effort to any undertaking. They are never pleased and never worried, nor can they ever be persuaded of anything. They are imperturbable, because they are not afraid of suffering. Light-bulbs too do not weep when they are switched off; cables do not attempt to avoid short circuits and firewood does not flee from the flames.

The inhabitants of the city might well envy the stones their freedom, if they were capable of perceiving it. Yet they too, though they do not know it and do not wish to, besides the ephemeral life of their bodies and minds, contain within themselves the indestructible life of stones. Whereas that which they themselves call their life turns out to be a fever eating away at their thoughts, which are tormented by the perpetual movements of sand, the powerlessness of clay, and the troubling plash of water. The inhabitants of the city want nothing to do with the life of stones, the only life that is in fact given to them. They are repelled by the stony calm of walls, and especially the certainty of the stone hand, which never trembles; by the firmness of features that never know sorrow and by the cold indifference of the monolith. The world of silence that endures inside the stones and the bricks, a world devoid of thoughts, feelings or desires, astounds and frightens them. And life without desires seems even more unbearable than the life without fulfillments that is experienced every day by many an inhabitant of the city.

Stupefied by the muddle of signs covering the walls, they miss the questions that dwell within the walls themselves. Those to which any answer is sufficient yet that nevertheless must remain unanswered, since they are stacked upon one another, forever joined by the cement of convictions. The answers to the questions that appear in the posters are attached to them with string, like a label on an item for sale secured additionally by a lead seal. The greatest number of questions are imprisoned within a desire. They ride up and down, like an elevator rattling the cage of its shaft. Or they roll along between two sidewalks like an abandoned ball, bouncing first one way then another, ever more slowly. Those that are light as down float in the air and are blown away on the wind. Everywhere there are multitudes of them, though no one needs them. But there is a shortage of questions that easily cut through space in search of answers. The city built of questions that have lost their momentum, and of routine answers, contains nothing that surprises or captures the attention. It is obvious that memory has nothing to latch on to here.

Each route is driven by trams bearing now one number, now another. In the middle of the street there suddenly appears a scrap-metal warehouse with boarded-up windows. It sometimes happens that the same place cannot be found twice, because the layout of streets has changed overnight. An elegant passage may suddenly become a foul-smelling blind alley; a luxury hotel will turn into a homeless shelter. This city is so dislocated that its Paris – a place about which all that is known is that they cannot make silk purses out of sows' ears there – has been transformed into a trash heap combed by hobos. An old umbrella with twisted spokes juts from it instead of the Eiffel Tower.

But in a city like this, even if it were made of gold and platinum and encrusted with diamonds, every precious building would still be merely a repository of disquiet; columns of wrongly posed questions would support arches of unserviceable answers and every door, without exception, could turn out to be the worst possible exit. And even if the city were constructed entirely of brand-new bricks and fresh plaster, pipes without a trace of rust, spotless windows and sidewalks glistening like mirrors, it would still remain a cage and a prison.

Like the countless reflections of an invisible dust mote in a kaleidoscope, there will multiply the numbers of Left Bank Parisian bistros in which girls in low-cut dresses lean over cups of black coffee with French novels in their hand. Red lightbulbs will shine over a street corner evidently detached from the Soho district of London, with garishly lit signs in English. In place of the pissoirs there appears a smoke-filled pub in which Irish poets drink, sing and play darts, while fanatical terrorists in army jackets plant time bombs. The place of the post office is taken by a New York drugstore where at four in the morning a pale theater critic suffering from a migraine will call in for sleeping pills. In the closed-down stocking repair shop there can be found a Palermo ice cream parlor in which taciturn men in shades will stare for hours at the glass door, pistols thrust beneath their jackets. At the newspaper kiosk brightly colored paper lanterns will light up while inside there will appear long rows of tables covered with tablecloths, on which dishes of snake and monkey meat will be served. Forever trapped in this city and occupying within it less space than a bookmark,

Palermo, Belfast and Hong Kong also go to rack and ruin, and fragments of them are found in ever different and more unexpected places.

Names also ebb away. Erosion has polished the letters; some it has crumbled and scattered. Those that remain no longer have any substance. It is a pity that the name vanishes. Yet could it be as beautiful as it is if it did not disintegrate from one moment to the next? When there are no letters there is no city. For only they were something certain in the chaos of dates, events and imaginings. Only they encompassed that which could not be encompassed: joyous First of May parades, and the forgotten helicopters of the municipal transit system, which from having flown for so long without fuel have also shrunk and apparently now hover low over the ground in the botanical gardens in the guise of dragonflies.

A rickety enclosure made from a handful of letters, amongst which there jut out the spikes of *W*s and *A*s, now has to contain air-conditioned American banks, cruel and ruthless arms dealers, illegal manufacturers of heroin who shoot at the police from behind chewing-gum kiosks, shivering Gypsies squatting on the sidewalks, and Asian women selling French perfumes on the street directly from suitcases. It may be that at some point supercilious Cossacks in armored personnel carriers will surround the city's central intersection, or that the savage hordes of Genghis Khan will pitch their tents and build campfires along the main thoroughfare, blocking the way for the trams and buses full of people on their way to work. It may be that Tartar warriors will start slaying passersby with blows of their spiked clubs. But they too will be unable to prevent the collapse of the whole.

There is no one who might know what to do with the damaged construction. It has become clear that the polishing of floors, the cleaning of sidewalks, the spraying of water on the asphalt on hot days or even the painting of walls with oil paint – none of this was sufficient; but the inhabitants of the city did not know how to do more. Disheartened they neglect their duties, which are of an ancillary nature and of little significance. The essence of the city was and remains incomprehensible; if the city planners had some vision of it they kept it to themselves, perhaps in the hope that this knowledge would never be needed. The inhabitants of the city know how to repair only that which can be touched. They are unable to touch that which cannot be seen and yet is most impaired, and that which has an indirect influence on the condition of the whole, since it controls the flow of nouns, adjectives, verbs, affirmative and negative sentences. The true indicators of urban solutions are the utterly unknown rules of joining sentences and creating stories, the principles of linking ideas with other ideas and of assigning weight to questions and answers.

In the current state of affairs streams of groundwaters, strata of clay, and sandbanks are a constant threat to the city. If purity is to be maintained in the enclosed region of happiness that the city was meant to be – this bastion of order holding back the stormy ocean of chaos – then sentences and stories must be removed to the outside day and night, as is done by the municipal sewers, so that in the city there should not remain a speck of dust, not a puddle, not an ounce of trash on the squared paper of the sidewalk. Even words need to be removed. But then that which remained in the city would be dispersed in a single instant in the waters of the countercity, like a flotilla of ships that have lost their anchors.

The inhabitants feel they have been cheated. Irked and embittered, they ask why the creators of the plans did not ensure that the foundations were properly separated from the bedrock: in other words why they were not placed in the air, far from any sources of rot and decay. But the creators of the plans say nothing. Is it possible that they too have been swallowed up by oblivion? Is it possible that they never really existed? Then whose will and whose views are imprinted in the framework of the city? No one knows. Those who ask must seek an answer on their own. One possible answer declares that attempts were indeed made to put the foundations in the air, but that the inertia of liquid concrete proved an obstacle: its boundless indifference and the fact that for its part it did nothing to support order. The stubborn passivity of building materials is responsible for the fact that the city could not realize the hopes placed in it.

The greater the regularity and harmony beneath the sealed dome of the sky covering the buildings and streets, the greater the confusion on its far side. There in the blue depths, whirling in disorder, is all that was ever successfully removed from the city: faulty castings, chipped sandstone slabs, fragments of red brick, umbrellas snatched away by the wind, wood shavings and sawdust, empty cigarette packets and mountains of butts, streams of engine oil, moldering herringbone caps, rags, potato peelings, roiling clouds, excrement, and even the twisted spans of bridges. And though the dome of the sky protects the city from a meteor storm or an inundation of trash, it still finds its way into the groundwaters and by this route returns.

Just as unattainable as absolute airtightness, it seems, is complete purification. In essence it is necessary to remove thoughts before they even arise. For in this city there are no thoughts other than confused ones, nor any events but accidental ones. It is never clear which thought was the source of things that happen, or how it managed to move the mechanical components of the world to set the event in motion. There is no way to determine whether thoughts are the consequence of accomplished facts or their cause, the product of a familiar machinery or that which lends direction to the movement of its cogs.

Unfortunately nothing is known about how the cogs themselves are made or of what, well hidden as they are from sight. Initial confidence in their high quality was so great on the building sites that they were installed without being inspected. It was quite another story with the lime that was mixed on the spot: Anyone could see that it was lumpy. Those who employed it relied on the perfection of the principal construction, believing that it could withstand anything. They counted on its boilers, engines and gears being without exception of the finest quality; they were simply indestructible. With use it became apparent that the unseen components of the world had also been made carelessly and of low-grade materials, worse even than the defective bricks with which the inhabitants of the city had raised their shaky edifices.

The special mechanisms separating good from bad became completely overgrown with the de-aeration and purification machinery that worked exclusively to serve their needs. It was said that these mechanisms themselves created more chaos than they were able to pump out beyond the dome of the sky. When the authors of the idea of cutting off the city from the countercity reduced all problems to the matter of the power supply for the mechanisms, they could not have foreseen how costly it would prove to continually remove all disorder from the world. For is the world not composed of disorder?

With the passage of years the artificially stretched thoroughfares of the city began to droop. Gaps and concrescences began to appear, and even stress fractures in all kinds of installations, including the most important ones, those involved in the removal of the countercity. Filth accumulated in the city. Soot stuck to the plaster, a wooly substance gathered in the seams of the inhabitants' clothing and the window ledges and cornices were covered with bird droppings. Cats tore mice to pieces in shadowy corners. Stairwells acquired the cat-and-mouse smell of that which is dark, random and cruel. All objects turned gray, just like the *W*s and *A*s in the name of the city. At some unknown moment the glints in windowpanes vanished. Crystal chandeliers lost their luster. Though in fact the majority of them had been taken down when they became hazardous. Gilding peeled from the frames of mirrors, the plush upholstery of armchairs grew worn and even the red of the tramcars faded. The sides of canals were coated with a greasy slime. Walls subsided; pavements collapsed.

Here for example is a street on which it is always raining. No one knows what pipe runs above it or why it burst. Streams of water pour onto the roofs of the apartment buildings, flow down the windows and gather far below between the façades. Cars move along the roadway as if it were the bottom of a deep canal, where it is dark and greenish and umbrellas sprout like algae. The passersby find it hard to breathe, as happens under water. Mothers drag small children on their daily route from store to playground. Not inclined to sentimentality before dinner is ready, they no longer pay any attention to the suffering of their own lungs, accustomed to the fact that everything immersed in this water manages to go on living. At dusk the tenants sail away on the current to distant bodies of water that only they know. Their thoughts begin to tip one way and then the other, unstable boats without a crew. No one maintains these boats; every one of them has something missing, and the brightly colored fish of coral reefs swim amongst wrecks that are already lying on the ocean floor. At times a sea horse swims up to a window ledge, working its little snout, or a wave carries some fish behind a wardrobe.

There is also a street that is enveloped in cold separated from heat, the way that in other places ravines are enveloped in morning mist. The cold separated from the heat turns into ice all around – ice that is so icy that all the coal in the world would not be enough to melt it. On the perpetually frost-covered windowpanes there grow together and then descend toward the ice-strewn roadway soaring gates, magnificent ice arches, sky blue, purple and white galleries, hanging bridges and glassy mountains that fill the entire space of the street. The delicate yet strong construction enwraps roofs and gutters and eats into the walls of buildings. For this reason the street is closed to traffic and special road signs direct drivers to a detour. But the inhabitants of the ice-bound apartments fall into a profound sleep right after dinner and dream that they have frozen to death.

The heat separated from the cold must also gather somewhere. An excess of heat makes the underground installations boil over. Thus there is a street in the city on which high temperatures have not ceased even for a moment for many years. The grass there has dried up and turned to dust that is blown into clouds by the torrid wind. Dust specks fly into people's eyes, making the whites bloodshot; this in turn gives their faces an expression of suppressed rage. Sand gets everywhere, ruining clocks and sewing machines. At night shouts are heard and the red glow of cigarettes flares in the entranceways of buildings. It is so hot that no one is able to fall asleep. Some there have gone for years without slumber, growing ever more irritable. Under every street lamp there stands a drunk and a prostitute and every ten minutes an ambulance or fire truck goes by, its siren wailing. In kitchens cabbage fried in lard is burned to the pan; children run in front of trams; young women put garish lipstick on mouths black with curses; burglars escaping over the rooftops fall onto the sidewalk and smash their skulls. Later, during the autopsies sand is found in their hearts.

In yet another place an excess of clay has accumulated. Every year after winter the apartment buildings subside into the miry earth. The lowest floors were the first to disappear. The inhabitants realized that there was no hope for them there and moved to suburban villas with ivy-covered turrets. In this way the swamp ceased forever to pose a threat to them. But it swallowed a living part of the city which – like rebellious tissue – began to grow downward. Hoists bring clay up to the surface to make room for successive floors. Apartments, stores, shops and parking garages wait to be occupied by those who are unable to find their place. Spent light bulbs burn there. Lathes without blades, sewing machines without needles and cranes without pulleys operate day and night.

The most dangerous emergencies cannot be eliminated, nor can further disasters be avoided. Yet the city will grow accustomed to anything. The sky of movable clouds drops lower every year, but till it starts to crush the roofs no one spares it a thought. It is not inconceivable that even the most important part of the machinery, that which turns the sky of fixed stars and above it the sky of suns and moons, is nothing but a pile of junk. It is not known exactly what it was made of or how. It may be that the plans are still stored in the archives, but there is no one who is able to decipher them. It can only be very roughly guessed which installations were set in motion overhead above the rooftops and which were put in underground. To this day some of those who mixed the mortar, carried the bricks and bent the pipes are still alive. But they know nothing except that in the beginning they labored hard and did not spare themselves. One or another of them can even show a hand missing fingers that were cut off by a chainsaw, the stump of a leg crushed by a block of stone, a scarred hole in the skull. They remember only themselves, in scraps of memories, scurrying about sun-drenched building sites in pants spattered with lime.

If they were to build the city again the main thoroughfares perhaps would run through the admissions room of a hospital, the halls of train stations would contain immense dormitories, and trams would drive along their tracks into the river. For there is no one here who could control the chaos of the countercity, no one who knows the laws that give truly accurate estimates, no one who knows how to prop the sky up, no one who could tell the bricklayers and architects what to do. There exists no knowledge better than ours, no building materials better than ours, and no way out better than the worst. The belief that the city could be different was not borne out. The juices that gave it life at the beginning of the season of vegetation have dried up. The choral songs have sounded their last and have fallen silent. No brick is passed any longer from hand to hand; the lenses of the twin-lens reflex cameras with which the sunny building sites were once photographed are covered with dust and have clouded over in dark drawers, useless because they no longer let in light. In these days of the world's old age everyone here is alone, and everyone has their own city which showers them with crumbling plaster, dead leaves and the dust of worn-out words.

On cold sleepy mornings blood stops flowing in the veins, the eyes can barely see and people lack the strength to take the next step. Nurses, seamstresses, fitters and chauffeurs, barely alive, doze off on the stairs holding onto the banister. At times someone opens their eyes all of a sudden and begins to look around, finding nothing familiar anywhere and amazed at how close it is from the youth of the world to its old age. And they cannot understand where the mistakes of youth have gone to, the outbursts of feeling, the songs. What has become of the new path of life: Could it possibly have turned into this exhausting, steep, lonely, cobweb-strewn path up and down the stairs? Where is the joy of the parents whose infant sat up in the baby carriage for the first time one warm afternoon, now, all these years later, when everything is already known about advancements, promotions, accidents, divorces and funerals?

The work of creation would have remained incomplete had it not been rounded off with a flood. The countercity had long ago burst its dams. Like a stormy sea that in a single instant pours over the laboriously reclaimed polders, it inundated the entire city from its foundations to its rooftops. When did the leaks begin? No one remembers. It may have been in the first minute after construction began. The river that flows through the city, bearing shattered, glittering reflections of soaring bell towers and steep roofs, merges its waves with the stagnant green waters of memory. And both waters, the one and the other, dissolve like a single droplet in the sea in the black waters of oblivion. For the countercity no water is ever too green or too black. That bottomless ocean receives it all unconditionally, always and in any amount, to the last drop.

Some blame everything on the fine palace that stands in the center of the city. They say it is too tall and that its needle made the first scratch on the sky. Yet in the kitchens that can be seen from its highest floors, no one complains any longer. They are deserted, as if they had been emptied by the plague. At times in the night someone will pass through them and briefly turn on a light. Those who once believed that what is pure will be ever purer and later discovered that purity turns into dirt now rebel against the requirement of absolute impermeability. They whisper that nothing is dirty only when nothing is pure. They want to allow everything that for years with the greatest effort was removed beyond the dome of the sky to mingle with the substance of the city. They assert that if the desire for perfection is only abandoned, then permeability will cease forever to threaten us.

Then the upper and lower waters, once separated, will join together again; the upper waters will cease pouring down on roofs while the lower waters will cease washing away foundations. At that time too, calm will come to the great stormy ocean, on whose waves the sailors of brick-built ships fight for their lives and drown and sink to the bottom like stones, not knowing that life cannot be lost. Drowning sailors do not remember which port they were headed for. Relinquishing unrealistic goals, they can give themselves entirely to the waves and know relief. One way or another all of them – including those who have already come to rest on the bottom – will return safely home.

It is said that neither more beautiful dreams nor another easier life will be of any use to us. It may be that all we need is an even greater turmoil of ever more ardent desires, ever more troubling questions and ever more vapid answers, whose random selection like gambling without prizes brings only torment. Yet torment too cannot last forever: It always moves toward breaking point. There is hope that the glare from which the eye loses all ability to distinguish colors and shapes will turn into the banal image of a street corner, a sign above a store, lace curtains in a window: a sight from which nothing transpires. The uproar from which the ear loses all ability to distinguish sounds will be transformed into the mild silence of waking life, the same silence that endures inside stones. The crushing pressure of thoughts that make the head throb with pain will in the end reveal a light, transparent void.

May that void unfold inside every brick and permeate everything in the world: buildings, sun and stars, clouds in the sky, air in the lungs and the lungs themselves. Only then will the palm begin to fit the handle of the tool, the hat fit the head and the rib cage cease to separate the heart from the rest of the world. Then it will be easier to accept the obvious truth that the burden oppressing us weighs nothing at all. The city to which the tree of the world gave birth at the beginning of this story is not real, just like the tree and like us ourselves. But the life of stones, which has no care for the past or the future, existed and will continue to exist: a steadfast endurance free of any name.

Our immense thanks to Anibal Joao Melo,
Janis Frame, and Jeffrey Lependorf, whose generous
support made this first paperback printing possible.